W9-CXV-975

Theories of Relativity

Barbara Haworth-Attard

THEORIES OF RELATIVITY

Harper *Trophy* Canada®

An imprint of HarperCollins *Publishers Ltd*

Theories of Relativity
© 2003 by Barbara Haworth-Attard.
All rights reserved.

No part of this book may be used or repro-
duced in any manner whatsoever without
the prior written permission of HarperCollins
Publishers Ltd., except in the case of brief
quotations embodied in reviews.

First edition

HarperCollins books may be purchased for
educational, business, or sales promotional use
through our Special Markets Department.

HarperCollins Publishers Ltd.
2 Bloor Street East, 20th Floor
Toronto, Ontario, Canada
M4W 1A8

www.harpercanada.com

National Library of Canada Cataloguing
in Publication

Haworth-Attard, Barbara, 1953–
Theories of relativity / Barbara Haworth-Attard.
– 1st ed.

ISBN 0-00-639299-7

I. Title.

PS8565.A865T44 2003   jC813'.54
C2003-903275-2
PZ7

HC 9 8 7 6 5 4 3

Printed and bound in the United States
Set in Monotype Plantin Light

For my niece, Melissa Haworth,
who first said, "I have a theory . . ."

Chapter 1

I have a theory that every fourth person will give me money. Like any good theory, mine is based on experimentation and observation. It's time-consuming, but it's not like I have anything better to do.

I'm sitting on a low cement wall set close to a glass-sided office tower. My backpack, with a sleeping bag tied to the bottom, is wedged behind me. Safe. A small concrete pool is in front of me. In summer, high arcs of water shoot white foam against a blue sky and people sit here to eat their lunch. But now it's November and the fountain is turned off. Yellow leaves fill the pool, and cold winds keep people away. Except me. I sit here and ask for money. Every day. Soon the tower doors will open and the first of the lunch crowd will trickle out. In the meantime, a woman pushing a baby stroller comes toward me.

"Spare change?" I ask. More from habit than expectation. She's person number one. The woman avoids my eyes and steers the stroller wide of me. I feel she's alert, scared I might jump up and grab her baby. Maternal instinct in high gear. My mother would have given me away for pocket change—or less.

A weak shaft of sun pierces the lowering grey sky and slides down the side of the tall brick building opposite, then wavers and disappears. I grimace and push my hands deep into my pockets. I need a heavier coat.

Person number two is a balding man in a grey suit, overcoat unbuttoned, tails flapping importantly behind. A cyclone of gold and red leaves swirls about him, stirred up by his hurrying feet. His body is tilted slightly to one side by the weight of his briefcase. Lawyer. "Anysparechange?" It's only a token question. He is, after all, a lawyer. He passes without a glance.

Person number three barrels from the tower at a trot. She left early to hit the pizza shop, I'm guessing. The line for that place can stretch two blocks. Worth the wait, though. Best pizza in the world: herb tomato sauce, spicy pepperoni, long strings of melting cheese. My stomach growls. It doesn't help that the sausage vendor is firing up his grill next to the dead fountain. The woman draws level with me.

"Do you have any spare change?" I feel a slight hope. There are dark half-circles under my eyes and women are sympathetic.

"Sorry," she throws over her shoulder as high heels click her away.

It was only a slight hope. Number four is coming from the tower. A man in his early thirties, slight build, khakis, beige shirt, no tie, bomber jacket, glasses. I like to think I can label anyone these days, and this guy is definitely a technical support geek.

These tech guys are nerdy but flush with cash. I hear women really go for them. I'd like to be flush with cash and have women plaster themselves all over me. I hold out my hand and debate smiling, then go for the cold, pleading look instead. "Any spare change for a hot drink?" I ask.

He stops. "I work for my money, you know."

That takes me aback. It's usually the middle-aged guys, bellies straining shirt buttons, foreheads creased with the realization that half their lives are gone and the next half won't be any better, who say that to me. They jab a finger at me as they talk. "I work for my money." *Jab.* "I don't sit around expecting a free ride." *Jab, jab.*

"You should be in school getting an education, so you can get a job," he says. "You can't live all your life on handouts."

Thank you, number four, for blowing my theory all to hell. I don't answer. Silence usually makes the finger-jabbers go away. They want confrontation.

This one doesn't leave, and that pisses me off. The church tower will soon chime twelve times, and for ten minutes I'll have a steady stream of people to part from their money as they rush past on their way to lunch. This do-gooder preacher in front of me will keep them away. I sink back onto the wall and lower my head. A grey pigeon pecks at a crust of bread on the ground. If I had seen it first, I would have fought that bird for it. I stare at the tips of the guy's shoes, black sneakers. Eventually, they turn and leave.

I look up to see that Jenna has arrived across the street at the Holy Rosary Cathedral. She's late this morning.

"Hi, Dylan," she calls to me.

She places a basket on the sidewalk outside the black iron gate, then sits beside it. Jenna's half-starved frame—*waiflike,* fashion people would call it—is a big hit with the lunch crowd. Add her white-blond hair, mournful blue eyes, and tremulous lips, and people fall over themselves to give her money. She's new to the street. Been here— I wrinkle my forehead and search my brain. It's hard to keep track of time, but I think she's been here for six days.

The office tower is my turf. The church is her turf, or rather Vulture's turf. He's striding up the street right now, anger in every line of his body. His real name is Brendan, but that's too wimpy for a ruthless bird of prey. He's a scavenger, picking away at people's bones for every bit he can get. A vulture. Dollar signs replace his eyeballs, just like in cartoons, when he sees Jenna. She's a money-maker.

He shouts at her, mad she wasn't there earlier. He yanks off her hat, takes her gloves and coat. She tries to grab the jacket back, then quickly subsides. No one gives money to a warmly dressed street kid. He tugs her long hair out of its elastic band and she grabs her head. That must have hurt. Jerk. Arranging the blond hair to frame her face, Vulture places a small blue blanket around her shoulders and tilts her head slightly downward. I suddenly realize what he's done. He's recreated every picture I've ever seen of the Virgin Mary. All he needs is a baby to place in her lap to complete the look. If she stays on the street long enough, she'll provide him with that, too.

He stands back, an artist critically examining his work, then leans forward and pushes her shoulders into a droop. I hate him, but I have to admire this bit of business. Fresh from noon Mass, people will leave the church, hearts overflowing with charity, to find the Madonna smack in front of them.

"Here."

It's the nerd with the black sneakers.

"You look like you need this." He thrusts a sausage on a bun at me.

I don't know what to do. The church bells have finished ringing the noon hour. In office cubicles throughout the tower, people will gather up purses and thrust arms into coats. They will push the button for the elevator and tell jokes as they count down the floors, then they will surge through the glass doors. To me. I can't ask for money while stuffing my face. Yet my stomach insists I have that sausage.

"Thanks," I mutter as I take it. I wonder what he wants. That's another of my theories. No one gives something for nothing.

But he merely nods and leaves.

The bun is warm and soft. Fragrant. My mouth fills with saliva until I'm drooling like the Garbage Man, the psycho who wanders the streets wearing green garbage bags. There's a ton of crazies living out here. I steer wide of them. Most are harmless, but occasionally you run up against one who's not. Besides, I sort of worry their craziness might be catching, like the flu.

I sink my teeth into the spicy sausage. There's onions and sauerkraut on it. I can't get it into me fast enough. People flow from the building and part around me. Mouth full, I can't panhandle. My jaws work frantically, but not fast enough, and I've lost the lunch crowd. I'm so stupid.

A woman shoots me a startled look. I must have spoken out loud. First drooling, now talking to myself. "Any spare change?" I ask her.

She trips on a crack in the sidewalk in her haste to get away.

I lick grease from my fingers and wish I could eat the sausage all over again.

Vulture darts across the road to Jenna, scoops up some change from the basket, and leaves. It doesn't do to have too much money. It's a fine balance. Too many coins and people stop giving; no coins and they don't give.

Gloomily, I picture the stack of money Vulture has made from Jenna. But at least my theory still holds. Number four came through—even if it was just a sausage.

Chapter 2

Jenna dodges a cab and crosses the street to flop down beside me.

"A good day," she says. "Brendan had to come twice to get the money. How did you do?"

I shrug. I have a theory that the best way to communicate is with a shrug. By raising and lowering your shoulders, you can speak volumes. But the real benefit is that every person interprets a shrug to his or her own satisfaction. I shrug and Jenna thinks I've done okay, because that is what she wants to believe.

A gust of wind spins into a mini tornado of dirt and dead leaves that dances down the road and throws grit into our faces.

"Shit." Jenna shields her face.

"You'd think when they put these office buildings on opposite sides of the street, they'd have known the wind would funnel between them," I say.

"Who?" Jenna asks, bewildered.

"The architects, engineers. They have wind tunnels to test this kind of stuff."

She looks at me like I'm an alien. I feel my shoulders begin to rise, but I lower them. Why shrug? There's only one inter-pretation she could put on me—lame.

A second blast of wind whips Jenna's hair about and, when it passes, leaves a silver tendril across the back of my hand. Feather-soft, it burns my skin. My thoughts fly back to when I was a kid, at my grandparents' farm, a butterfly on the back of my hand, delicate pearl-white wings opening and shut-ting. I couldn't believe that something so fragile trusted me.

"It's getting cold," Jenna says. She pulls her coat taut across her breasts.

"Frost on the pumpkin tonight," I say absently. My mind is full of her hair on my hand and butterflies—and her breasts.

"Huh?"

Yup, I'm definitely lame. "Just something my grandfather used to say. It means it's going to be really cold tonight. He had a farm. He was a farmer," I finish weakly.

Jenna turns her head to look down the street. "Trouble coming."

I follow her gaze to a police officer sauntering toward us.

"Let's go." She jumps off the wall and walks rapidly in the opposite direction. I grab my backpack, check that my sleep-ing bag is securely tied to it, and jog after her.

"What's the rush?" I ask.

"My parents have probably filed a missing person's report." Her voice is muffled by her coat collar. She turns a corner and grabs my arm. "In here."

She yanks me into the deep-fried warmth of Mandy's Donuts. Everyone who lives on the street ends up here at some point. It's the only place that will put up with us—as long as we don't make trouble and occasionally buy some-thing. I don't know if there is a Mandy.

We slide into the booth farthest from the street. Jenna unzips her coat and shakes her hair free. I can smell it, freshly washed. She stayed somewhere last night that had hot water. In the three weeks I've been out here, I've washed my hair only once. In horror, I shrink back in the booth. If I can smell her, she must be able to smell me. And I stink! I vow that today I will have a good wash at the library bathroom. It didn't matter a whole lot until now.

"Want anything?" she asks.

I shake my head. "I'm not hungry," I lie.

"My treat," she says, and smiles. Her face lights up like there's a hundred-watt bulb inside her.

My heart melts. "Fries and a Coke, then," I croak.

The sign says Mandy's Donuts, but they serve everything: bacon, eggs, hamburgers, fries, and, yeah, donuts.

I watch Jenna walk up the aisle, lean over the counter, and charm the clerk. Acne-faced jerk. All he does is dip frozen fries into hot fat, take money, and say *Have a good day*, but I can't even get that job. I know because I tried.

"You don't look clean enough," the owner said. "This is food you're working around."

A few minutes later, Jenna walks back, balancing two drinks and fries piled high in cardboard containers. Charm obviously works.

I grab ketchup and vinegar and, for good measure, squirt mustard and relish over the fries. It's all food.

"So, you think your parents have reported you missing?" I ask. The fries are hot and fresh.

"Well, Brendan says they probably did. He says I should watch out for police and social services. I'm sixteen in a couple months, so then it won't matter. He says they can't touch me once I'm sixteen. He watches out for me."

Vulture watches out for his investment. But I know what she means. When you first land on the street, you're so shit-scared you latch onto whatever security you can find. For me, it was a girl, Amber, who took me under her wing. Also Vulture's property, I soon found out. People like Vulture know a new street kid is vulnerable and they take advantage of it. I've always had to look out for myself, so I saw right through him and kept out of his clutches. But I'm not stupid. I stay out of his way.

Jenna sticks a straw through the plastic top of her drink. "What about you? Are your parents looking for you?"

"I doubt it," I tell her.

"Why not? Won't they be worried about you? Do your mother and father live together?"

That last question surprises me. Out here, we don't press each other for our stories, our background. Amber told me that. "We might be curious," she said, "but we give each other our privacy." It's a sort of rule. Jenna hasn't been on the street long enough to know that.

My fingers search the cardboard container, but I've finished the fries. I squirt ketchup over my fingers and lick it off. I'm never full. I think it was one of the reasons I had to leave—or, rather, why my mother kicked me out. Jenna's a runaway, but I'm a throwaway. Tossed out. Like garbage.

"Well, I'm sort of between fathers right now," I say. "There's been three of them. All losers. Especially my biological father. His name's Phil, but I've never met him."

"You've never met your father?" She looks incredulous. "And there's two others?"

What would she say if I told her about the uncles sandwiched in between? I study her again: the coat, the designer jeans, the sweater. Real money. I'm envious and scornful, but at the same time, I feel a pang of fear for her. No wonder she fell into Vulture's arms. Her comfortable world was light-years from mine, yet she ran away from it. I was forced from my world. She can always go back. I can't. I tried. Two weeks ago I pleaded with Mom to let me back into the house. She said no.

I open my mouth to say my mother's a whore, but what comes out is, "My mother has trouble making the right choices." Shit, I sound like an afternoon talk show. Heat rises in my face.

"What about your grandfather? The 'pumpkin' man. Or do you have three of them, too?" She grins, and that beaming face makes me forgive her for her easy life.

"Just the one," I tell her. Though there might be another. Mom never talked about her parents. They could be dead for all I know.

"My mother and father were teenagers," I tell Jenna. "She was in school until she got pregnant. Just turned sixteen. My father was a year older. When he found out Mom was pregnant, he told the principal to put his head where the sun don't shine and went off and got drunk for a week. He never showed up for my birth and he left town soon after. End of story." Shredded cardboard, all that's left of the container, sits in a small pile on the table in front of me.

Jenna nods, but her eyes rove around the shop, and I sense she's anxious to leave. I want her to stay, so I keep talking. "My granddad was my real father's dad," I say. "He and my grandmother took care of me a lot." When Mom wouldn't or couldn't, or when the uncles came to stay. "They lived on a farm. Everything was huge there—the barn, the cows, the tractors, the field corn, and my granddad. He was huge, too." And suddenly I can see him clearly: tall, barrel chest under a flannel shirt, monster hands pushed into worn work gloves. "I followed him everywhere. All over the farm." And I felt safe.

"When Pete came, Mom wouldn't let me go to the farm any more." I'm babbling. "Pete is my brother Jordan's father. Granddad came to the house to pick me up and Mom told him I wasn't there, but I was. Pete had his hand over my mouth. Granddad and Mom argued. She said since my father wasn't paying support, my grandparents should pay if they wanted to see me. Granddad said he'd take her to court. That's the last time I saw him. I bit Pete's hand."

I smile at the memory of him jumping around, shaking his hand, screaming and swearing. Not so funny is the memory of the bruises I carried around on my back for three weeks after.

I hated Pete. He and Mom would get drinking and then they'd fight. It always ended the same way—his fist laying her out on the floor. Then one day he hit Jordan, baby Jordan. She went all crazy and threw his stuff out the front door. That would have had curtains twitching in some neighbourhoods, but fights were so common where we lived, people didn't blink an eye.

I fiddle with the straw in my drink, thinking about Jordan. He's ten and showing every sign of becoming a major pain in the ass. Like his father. Mouthy at home, mouthy at school. Mom does nothing to stop it. So far, I've kept him out of trouble, but I'm not there now.

Jenna must be bored out of her mind. I tell myself to shut up, but my mouth motors on.

"I packed a bag one day. Thought I'd go live with Grand-dad. I took one step out the door and it was so black . . ." I catch myself. I almost told her how I was scared of night. Darkness. Still am. "I was just little. I didn't go."

Jenna nods and picks up her drink. As she does, her sleeve slides up to show a purple bruise on her inner arm, about the size of a man's thumb. She sees me looking and pulls down her sleeve. Her eyes slide over to the door. "Here's Brendan."

Vulture doesn't look happy as he comes up to us. His employee is eating his profits. I smirk into my drink.

He pushes in beside Jenna. She scuttles across the seat into the corner of the booth. She watches him with a wary, yet adoring, gaze. I want to kick her under the table and bring her back to reality. The guy is scum.

I've spoken to Vulture before, at Amber's apartment. He didn't like me being with her, and I can tell by his face he doesn't like me being with Jenna, either.

He takes off his coat to reveal camouflage fatigues and a black T-shirt. Tattoos cover his arms so completely, little skin shows through. Greasy brown hair is pulled into a ponytail and a moustache droops from his lip. But it's his eyes I find most disturbing. Dark brown predator eyes. Calculating. Watching. He's not a street person. He just preys on them.

"Who bought all this?" Vulture waves a hand at the fries and drinks.

Jenna's eyes widen in alarm as she realizes her mistake.

"I did," I lie. I stare straight in his predator eyes. I read somewhere that if you look a person directly in the eyes and don't shift your own, it appears you're telling the truth. I'm good at lying. I've had a lot of practice with teachers and principals and other kids. Lying helps you survive in a new school every year.

"You had a good day?" Vulture asks me.

I shrug.

"I could help you make better money," he says. He wants me to join his little army of street kids and do his bidding. It pisses him off no end that I won't. I've had *invitations* from him before, though most people would call them threats.

"Time to go." I pull on my coat and tug on the sleeping bag to make sure it's securely attached to my backpack.

"There's a party tonight . . ." Jenna begins. She glances at Vulture.

He doesn't encourage her, but doesn't discourage her either, so she goes on. "Would you like to come?"

"No, thanks," I say. A party, a beer, a snort of coke, a joint, a night of warmth off the street and suddenly you're in Vulture's grip.

"No, thanks," I repeat.

Chapter 3

A blast of warm air strikes me as I stride purposefully into the library. I need to look like I belong here. I stand in front of the New Books section, my brain working out how to get to the washroom unnoticed. The entrance is on the right side of the Checkout desk, directly in view of the librarians. The woman at Returns catches my eye, then exchanges a glance with the security guard at his desk. He gives me a hard look from beneath bushy eyebrows. Really bushy eyebrows, like grey furry caterpillars. I grab the nearest book and head to the lounge area. Libraries are forgiving places. As long as nothing drastic happens, they'll let me stay.

I shrug off my backpack and settle into a chair. The usual collection of weirdos is here. Some mumble, some tremble, some sit passively for hours, but all possess the same bewildered air, like they were teleported from another planet and don't quite know where they've landed. It hits me that I am one of them now.

I wind the strap of my pack around my ankle. I've never expended so much energy protecting a single article as I do for this backpack, but everything I own is inside: my clothes, my music, a sliver of soap, a razor, a ratty toothbrush, photographs. I live in constant fear of losing me.

The security guard walks through the lounge. I flip the book over and read the title: *Albert Einstein: Father of the Theory of Relativity*. As the guard nears, I raise the book so he can see the title and know that only someone seriously serious about reading would choose a book this boring. My eyes pick out a line to read: *Einstein's theory deals with the concepts of space and time*. The guard passes. I peer from behind the book at the old man seated across from me. He stares intently at nothing. He could tell Einstein a thing or two about space.

I return to the book and study the picture of Einstein, the father of theories. I know who he is—a genius. You can get away with a lot if you're labelled a genius. You can be rude and people will say, "Don't mind him, he's a genius."

Clown hair sticks out from Einstein's head. If that's what a life of thinking and theories does to you, maybe I should give up my theories, or keep my hair short. He has a slightly befuddled expression on his face. The father of relativity would be right at home with the people in this lounge. Maybe they're all geniuses.

Drowsy from lack of sleep, I let my eyes close. A commotion opens them, and I grab my backpack. With an inward groan, I see something drastic about to happen. Twitch.

"Hiya, Dylan," Twitch calls loudly. He falls over the feet of the Space Man and into a portable bookstand that skitters across the floor. He scrambles after it, shoving spilled books into the shelves any which way. A man behind the Information desk cranes his neck to see what is going on.

"Twitch," I whisper harshly. "Get over here and sit down." I don't want to be thrown out of this oasis of warmth.

His feet fly everywhere as Twitch crosses the room. He

plops into the chair next to me, slumps, bounces into a sitting position, then flops back again. One leg jiggles a quick rhythm. Hands twist and turn, then reach to scratch the top of his head, his nose, his chin. There is something seriously wrong with Twitch. Medically wrong. He is never still.

I am tall and thin, but Twitch towers over me by yet another head. He's skeletal, skin stretched so tight over his skull, it's pale blue and transparent. It's as if his body is living off itself, consuming him from the inside out. This translucence and his clumsiness lend him a desperate air of vulnerability.

I note the bead of snot on the end of his nose, his more than usual frantic restlessness, and the darting eyes. He's high. We won't last five minutes here.

"What's happening?" he asks loudly.

"Quiet," I tell him. Then, "Not much."

"What's that?" Twitch grabs the book from my lap. He rifles through the pages and stops at the photo of Einstein. "Strange-looking dude," he comments.

That's rich coming from Twitch with his green tufts of hair, multiple rings through his ears, and a painful-looking bolt through an eyebrow. I'd never have all that hardware on my face. One look at a needle and my head turns all woozy.

"Why do you always come here, man?" Twitch asks. He tosses the book up in the air and catches it. Sets up to do it again.

"Stop that!" I whisper.

The book twirls in his fingers. "These people give me the creeps," Twitch says, pointing at the Space Man. "You should come to the youth centre."

"They don't bother me," I say. The youth centre is for

street kids under twenty-five. I've never been and I don't want to go. I'm not like them. I'm fine here with books and ideas and theories.

Out the library window, it's already dark, though it's only five o'clock. I hate the way night comes early in the fall.

Twitch tosses the book to me but throws it wide, and it slams on the floor. The Information man is standing now. I had hoped to sit here until the library closed at nine—it makes the time out on the street a little shorter—but Twitch won't last that long. I've been too kind to him. Well, not really kind, just not unkind. Most people are unkind to Twitch, so if you ignore him, he thinks you're being kind.

I pull on my coat and shift the pack onto my back. It's better if I leave. I don't want to get banned from the library. It's my only haven. As I pass through the gate, a siren wails. The guard bustles up, caterpillars lowered in disapproval. I realize I'm holding the Einstein book.

"Sorry. Forgot I had it." I shove the book in his hands and bolt out of the library, Twitch on my heels. I never did get my wash.

"Do you have any money?" Twitch asks.

"No," I tell him. Tonight it's the truth, but I'd tell him that anyway. Twitch doesn't want to feed his stomach, just his veins. I've seen his arms. Scars from cigarette burns run up one, and needle punctures down the other. The first put there by his stepfather, the other by Twitch himself—probably to forget the first.

"Where did you sleep last night?"

"I didn't," I say shortly.

I'd moved around all night, one step ahead of punks and police and social workers desperate to offer a bed at the men's shelter. I hear they make you say a prayer there. I don't know if that's true, but I don't think I could stand sixty men's voices intoning, *Now I lay me down to sleep* . . . When the first grey light of dawn hit the downtown buildings, I'd breathed a sigh of relief, wrapped myself in my sleeping bag, and slept in a store doorway until I was kicked out by the owner. It's always a scramble to find a place to spend the night. Sometimes I stay in the donut shop, nursing a coffee for hours. Once in a while, I'll crash on someone's couch. Twice I dozed in the park on a bench. But the worst nights are the ones where I wander downtown, freezing, wet, freezing, scared, freezing, exhausted.

"I know a guy who'll let us crash at his place," Twitch says.

"Why?" I ask.

"He's nice. He's got a great apartment."

I snort my disbelief. But a warm place, maybe a shower. I want so badly to believe this guy is just *nice.*

"We could go see him," Twitch suggests.

I can't face another night like the last one. Tears gather behind my eyes at the thought.

"Sure, we'll go see him," I tell Twitch. If it doesn't feel right, I can always leave.

Twitch walks a couple paces in front, turns to face me, then he's beside me, bouncing, always moving. He wears me out.

The *nice* guy lives in an old church converted into apartments, complete with wood trim, arched windows, and high ceilings. Whoever designed these places worked hard to keep the atmosphere. "Great place," I tell the nice guy, Brad.

Brad looked decidedly uneasy when he answered the door and saw me standing there. I don't blame him. I wouldn't have let me in, either. I'd worry that I'd steal myself blind.

After a long hesitation, he let us in. "Well, if you're a friend of Aaron's."

Aaron? That was Twitch's real name?

I run my hand over some wood panelling. "Is this from the original church?" I ask.

"Yes. Quite a bit of the woodwork is restored," Brad says, thawing visibly. "It dates from 1873." Brad is in his mid-forties, double-chin, slight paunch, hair slicked over a bald patch he's trying to outwit.

"Dylan likes buildings and stuff," Twitch chimes in. "He says the library is a classic. Especially the gargoyles over the doors."

Brad makes three cups of coffee and puts them and a plate of biscotti on a table between two small sofas. "Help yourself," he says.

And I do. Three cookies are rapidly washed down by hot, strong coffee. I've had no supper. I try to imagine myself with a job, coming home to a place like this, to coffee and biscotti.

"Want one?" Brad holds out a small box of pills, some blue, some yellow.

"No, thanks," I tell him. My muscles tense.

Brad nods and offers the box to Twitch, who eagerly takes two pills. Brad pops one himself, then closes the box.

I relax, surprised that he didn't push them on me.

He puts on music and we sit. My eyes begin to close, but I force them open.

"Do you mind . . ." I begin. I hate asking people for favours. It leaves me obligated. "Do you mind if I have a shower? I have my own soap, and I won't use your towels or anything." I also hate that I'm pleading, but I'm desperate to be clean.

"No problem," Brad says. He points to a door. "Bath-room's through there."

I pick up my pack and go into a bedroom. Decorated in soft browns and creams, it's so tidy that I just want to sit there and let it bring order to my mind. My grandparents' place was like this.

Soon I'm in a glass-walled stall with hot water pouring over me. It feels so good, tears again gather behind my eyes. I shake my head, disgusted with myself. Wimp!

After a long while, I turn the water off and use a T-shirt to dry myself. I pull out my dirty clothes and sigh. It's gross putting them on my clean body, but I don't have anything else. I rinse out the stall to show Brad I'm not a pig and pass through the bedroom and into the living room.

"Thanks," I mumble.

Brads smiles but doesn't say anything, he's so mellow. Twitch sits on the floor, back against the sofa, and some-thing is different about him. I mull it over and then it dawns on me. He's not moving. I've never seen Twitch not move.

I stretch out on the floor inside my sleeping bag. As I drift off to sleep, I tell myself that I must find Jenna tomorrow, to show her what I look like clean.

Chapter 4

I dream a hand is on my thigh. Struggling from a deep sleep, I open my eyes and in one split second register the hand, the arm, the face. Brad.

"Get off," I yell.

I scramble to my feet, legs entangled in my sleeping bag. I kick it away, grab my pants, and pull them on.

"What the hell do you think you're doing?"

Brad cowers. "Sorry, man. I thought . . . maybe . . . I mean, you're with Aaron so I thought . . . ."

With Aaron. *With* Aaron. Twitch lies on the floor, so still I wonder if he's okay, but his chest rises and falls regularly.

"I would never force you, man," Brad says. "I'm not into that."

I want to hit something so hard. I turn and kick Twitch. No response. I kick him again, and this time his eyelids flutter.

"Asshole," I shout.

He blinks.

"You set me up, you asshole."

Twitch groans and runs a hand through his green hair.

"This guy had his fucking hand on my thigh." I feel sick. "You set me up."

"Brad's a nice guy." Twitch seems totally bewildered. He really doesn't know what I'm upset about.

Brad hurriedly retreats into his orderly bedroom and shuts the door. I roll the sleeping bag and tie it to my pack.

"Where are you going?" Twitch asks. "It's still night."

"I don't care. I'm not staying here." I pull on my coat.

"How can you do that?"

"Do what?"

"Do *that*. With him." I jerk my head toward the bedroom.

Understanding dawns on Twitch's face. He shrugs. "Brad gives me money. Food." His voice becomes flat. "You drink a bit, pop a pill, and it's not so bad. He's a good guy. And . . . you were warm here, right?"

And that makes it okay? "Just stay away from me," I tell Twitch.

I let myself out of the apartment into the early dark hours of a cold November morning. I turn my feet toward the donut shop, the only place I know for sure is open. A warm night. Maybe it does make it okay. I don't know any more.

A yellow school bus packed with kids passes where I sit outside the office tower. Seeing it reminds me that I never cleaned out my locker at school. It's been four weeks since I was there. Has anyone noticed my absence?

Jenna materializes in front of me. Deep shadows hollow her eyes, and her skin is blotchy.

"How was the party?" I ask.

She yawns hugely and flops down beside me. "It was okay for a bit, but then it got boring. Brendan went off with this other chick, Amber, so I got drunk. Real drunk," she adds.

The sun crests the office building, and light bounces off the glass into our faces.

"Oh, shit." Jenna winces. "That's bright."

Bright, but it is sunshine rather than rain! And Jenna is mad at Vulture. My spirits rise. "I'm going back to my old high school to clean out my locker. Do you want to come?"

"Brendan will want me at the church at noon," she says.

Other chick! Other chick! I send thought waves to her. *Dump him.* And it works.

"Yeah. Sure. Let's go. Let that *other* girl make his money for him today."

So she knows Vulture is using her. Why would she stay with him?

"We need bus fare," I say. "It's too far to walk."

"I'll get us some." Jenna tosses her hair, switches on her smile, and, like moths to a flame, people surround her. After a few minutes, she drops a handful of coins into my palm. "Bus fare and breakfast."

"It's yours." I hold the money out to her.

"No. Ours." She folds my fingers over the coins. "Let's go." She's checking the street both ways, fast losing her moment of bravado. I grab her hand before she changes her mind.

It's like a field trip. We sit at the back of the bus. Jenna pokes me with her finger every time I make her laugh and I love it. The bus lurches and she falls against me, soft and warm. She squeals and clutches my arm close to her chest, and my brain reels. Silver hair drifts across my face, and I'm pretty sure that's a breast beneath my elbow.

I'm not used to people being that close to me. Mom wasn't the touchy-feely type, like those television mothers. But then, I wasn't a cute television kid. Micha, my six-year-old brother, is, but Mom doesn't hug him, either. God, I miss him, his sticky fingers, his large brown eyes. And worry about him. He has nightmares, and I'm the one who holds him until he stops screaming. But I'm not there.

"What's the matter?" Jenna asks.

"I'm hungry," I lie.

"Let's get off then and have something to eat."

I thread my arms through my pack's straps and follow her rounded ass down the bus aisle and feel better.

We find a café smelling of yeast and coffee beans. If I worked there, I could breathe that air and the scent alone would fill me up. I wrap my hands around the cup and take a long pull of hot liquid. It warms me to my toes and gives my brain a jolt. "Why use blood for transfusions?" I joke to Jenna. "Just feed coffee into my veins." I want her to think I'm the funniest guy alive.

She stares at me. "You say the oddest things."

Why do I even open my mouth? I stuff my muffin into it, working on the theory that if it's busy, it can't say anything lame.

"So what were you really thinking about on the bus?" she asks.

Jenna's certainly not dumb—quite perceptive, in fact. Which makes her staying with Vulture all the more bizarre.

"My brothers," I tell her shortly.

As I cram the second half of the muffin in my mouth, I remember my brothers and me grossing each other out with chewed food. I swallow rapidly, afraid of grossing out Jenna.

"You told me about Jordan," she says. "You have another brother?"

"Yeah, Micha. He's six."

"Is Micha's dad your third father?" Jenna asks.

"Yeah. Harley. He was from Jamaica. A good guy." Anyone who doesn't use his fists to make conversation is a good guy in my books. "Pretty laid back." All that dope he smoked, he couldn't be anything but laid back, but he seemed to like us boys.

"He stayed about two years." The most peaceful time in my life outside of those short stretches I'd spent at my grandparents' farm. "Then welfare threatened to cut off our assistance because he lived with us, so my mother kicked him out." That's how she deals with problems. Out of sight, out of mind.

Jenna gets up to refill our coffee cups. I study the people in the shop. Some read newspapers; others stare into space, but not like the crazies at the library. These people have places, and people, and jobs to think about. I want to be one of them. I want to order a coffee, pay for it with money I didn't bum, open a newspaper, and worry about my job or the government raising my taxes.

"So you don't have a father at the moment." Jenna sits and places a cup in front of me.

"I might by now," I say. "There was this new guy she was interested in. Dan." I'd only seen him a couple of times through the window when he'd come to pick her up for a date. She didn't let him come into the house. Knew we'd scare him off. "So he might be living there, I don't know."

But he probably is. In my house. That was Mom's plan. She'd attracted a man who had a steady job. On and on she went about how respectable he was, which means he's probably a creep. Finally, she decided he should meet us kids. On my sixteenth birthday. Not that there was cake or balloons or presents.

"You're to tell him you all had the same father," she said to us boys.

I pointed at Micha, who is the colour of milk chocolate. "How are you going to explain him?"

She looked surprised, as if she'd just noticed that Micha's skin was much darker than ours. "We'll tell him there's Italian blood in the family."

I howled with laughter. "Italian blood! Micha's *black*, Mom. Like this guy's going to believe Micha's Italian."

Next thing I knew, Mom was shoving me toward the door and screaming, "Get out!"

I pushed back into the house, not believing she was serious, but she grabbed my backpack and began shoving my clothes into it.

"Where am I supposed to go?" I asked, grabbing the pack from her and cramming in a toothbrush, CDs, anything I could lay a hand on as she pushed me out of the bedroom.

"I don't care. You're old enough to get a job. I was living on my own at your age. Expecting you," she spat.

"Don't blame me for your lousy life," I shouted back. And next thing I know, I'm on the sidewalk, the door locked behind me, Micha's tearful face pressed to the window. Happy Birthday.

Chapter 5

I swagger down the school corridor. It's first lunch period and the halls swarm with kids. The guys are admiring Jenna, and she's with me, so I'm swaggering.

"They're not very friendly," Jenna says. "No one has said hello to you."

My swagger falters. "I was new here. No one knows me."

I've been to so many schools, I've lost count. Every eight to ten months, about the same amount of time it took a landlord to figure out we weren't paying rent, we moved.

I told Mom it wasn't good for Jordan or Micha to be the new kid all the time. Jordan "acted out," as one principal put it, and Micha had his nightmares. She told me to shut up. Couldn't I see she was making a new start and it would be different this time? She'd get a job, there would be food on the table, clothes on our backs. Ten months later, we'd move again.

I'm suddenly struck with an urgency to go to my brothers' school and see that they are okay. If they haven't moved. That thought hits so hard, I stop dead in my tracks.

Jenna has gone ahead, but now she turns and looks back. "What's wrong?"

"Mental block. Couldn't remember where my locker was.

It's here." I nod down the corridor that leads past the computer lab.

I like the computer lab. The computer geeks are so wrapped up in their hardware and software, they either ignore you or beg you to admire their latest programming feat. Any audience will do, even the new kid.

"Well, Dylan." Mr. Crowe, the computer teacher, comes out of the lab as we pass. He is short with dark brown hair that curls against his collar. I've never seen him in anything other than the clothes he wears now: a brown corduroy sports coat and tan baggy-kneed trousers. Clothes that make him appear more sparrow than crow.

"I called your home when you'd been absent a week, but the line's been disconnected," he says. He rocks on the balls of his feet, smiling broadly.

A spurt of fear knots my stomach, but then I remember Mom has never paid a telephone bill in her life. No doubt the service is cut off. I took care of the bills, promising payments to the gas, water, electricity, and phone companies that were never sent.

"I might have put down the wrong number." The words are barely out of my mouth when I realize my mistake. The phone number was on the form the *parent* was supposed to complete. "I mean, my mother did," I amend hastily.

Bright sparrow eyes stare at me steadily, showing he isn't fooled for a moment.

I take a couple steps to my locker and see the padlock is gone. I pull open the metal door to find it empty. "Do you know where my stuff is?" I ask.

"In the office."

Mr. Crowe beside me, and Jenna trailing behind, we walk

to the office. I'm not sure whether or not to introduce her. Probably not. She won't want to be singled out.

"Do you need help?" Mr. Crowe suddenly asks. "What's with the backpack and sleeping bag?"

"We're moving. I just brought my pack with me so it wouldn't get mixed up with my brothers' stuff. You know how a house gets turned upside down when you move." That sounds lame even to my own ears, but I look right at him as I say it.

"It takes you four weeks to pack?" Mr. Crowe stops at the office door.

"It's a big job," I say.

Jenna and I file into the office. Mr. Crowe stands at the entrance, blocking my escape. At least, that's how I see it. My leg muscles tense, ready to run.

"There are people who can help with situations like yours," he says.

I breathe in great angry gulps. What could he possibly know about my *situation*? I almost blurt that out, but that is exactly what he wants me to do. He is more the sly, black-feathered bird than I thought.

I struggle to keep my voice even. "I don't know what you mean. We're moving. I came to get my stuff."

Mr. Crowe leaves the door and comes around the counter, slaps a paper on its surface. "We'll need your new school's name and address so we can send them your records."

"I'm not registered yet. We're moving out west. Right across the country." That last bit is truly inspired. "I'll let you know as soon as I find out the school I'll be going to." He knows I'm lying, but too bad. There's nothing he can do. I'm sixteen. The law says a kid has to go to school until he's sixteen, though the truth is, once you turn fourteen, no one much cares if you go to school or not.

He reaches under the counter and brings up a box. It's my stuff. As he pushes it across to me, he turns to Jenna. "And what school do you go to?"

"Uh . . . I'm moving, too," she says.

"She's my cousin," I quickly add. "She's coming with us out . . ." and I can't remember if I said west or east, ". . . across the country."

Mr. Crowe raises his eyebrows, but I ignore him and rapidly sort through the contents: books, pencils, a pen, an ancient cereal bar and a towel that's more holes than cloth. It, the pen, and the cereal bar, go into my coat pocket. I shove the box and the rest of its contents back across the counter.

"Thanks."

I push Jenna out of the office, anxious to leave. "School," I say as we walk down the hall. "Who needs it?"

She looks wistfully at the kids in the cafeteria. "I didn't mind school so much," she says.

And suddenly I'm afraid she'll go back home. I'd miss her like hell. I've become used to seeing her face in front of Holy Rosary Cathedral. "You liked all that studying? Teachers telling you what to do?" I try to discourage her.

"It wasn't the teachers who were always telling me what to do." She pulls a face. "It was my parents. My father."

We leave the school and find ourselves in the smoking pit, the ground littered with cigarette butts and candy wrappers. Clouds cover the sun and a cold wind has sprung up. Knots of kids surround us, shivering, as they suck in smoke. A bell rings and butts are thrown away as students push past us and go into the school. The acrid scent of smoke lingers in the air. Mom smoked. She filled the house with blue clouds that clung to furniture and curtains and my clothes and hair. I couldn't escape the stink. It put me off so much, I've never even tried a cigarette.

"My dad is this complete control freak. He writes up rules for everyone in the house to follow," Jenna says. "And Mom just does whatever he says. She's so useless. I don't think she ever had an original thought in her life."

Abruptly, I'm tired. Jenna, face pinched with cold, looks worn out. The field trip is over.

"I better get back," she says. "Brendan will be looking for me."

"Does he have rules for you, too?" I ask.

"What?"

"Nothing. Do you have enough money for the bus?"

She nods.

"I'm going to go over to my brothers' school. I want to check that they're okay."

"Guess I'll see you around, then." She begins to walk away.

"Jenna," I call. "Do you have any brothers or sisters?"

She immediately comes back. "A sister. Why?" She sounds defensive, angry.

"No reason. Sorry." Now it's me breaking the privacy rule.

She punches me gently on the arm. "That's okay. I didn't mean to bite your head off. My sister's twelve." With a final wave, she leaves. She's mad at someone, but not me. I would have preferred a kiss to the jab on the shoulder.

It's a half-hour walk to Jordan and Micha's school. I gnaw on my thumbnail, playing different scenarios in my head. I will arrive at the school, but Jordan and Micha won't be there. I'll ask the school and they won't know where they've gone. My thumb is bleeding now. I whip it into my pocket and I tell myself to stop being a stupid drama queen. The school would know where. Wouldn't they?

I stop at a variety store and spend my bus fare on candy for Jordan and Micha. It'll be a long walk back downtown, but it's not like anyone's expecting me at a certain time. As I cram small bags of caramels and jelly beans in my pockets, I grin, picturing their faces when they see this haul. Micha will be on a sugar high for the rest of the day. My smile widens as I imagine Mom's face when she peels him off the ceiling.

I'm a few minutes early for the afternoon recess, so I sit on the climber. A blue car pulls up to the school door and a woman with a briefcase climbs out. Hair cropped tight against her skull, dressed in a dumpy coat. I recognize the type immediately—a social worker. We've had them at our house before.

Worry knots my insides. Is she there for Jordan or Micha? I have a theory about social workers. They're needy. They need to think they're bettering mankind. But they're really trying to make themselves feel good.

I was in a foster home for a bit, after Pete left, and Mom couldn't cope with me and a baby. Ever since I was returned to her, Children's Services have checked up on us. An appointment would be set up with Mom, and I'd kick out whichever father or uncle was living with us. The beer bottles would go after them. I'd hide the dirty dishes inside the oven, make the beds, and hold Micha and Jordan under water until the top layer of dirt came off. Then I'd hit the grocery store and buy—or, if the welfare cheque hadn't stretched to the end of the month, steal—a loaf of bread, and when the doorbell rang, I'd thrust Jordan and Micha into chairs at the kitchen table with plates of buttered bread. I'd open my textbooks and plop myself down in front of them. I was the director of a play called *Regular Family.*

The school doors open and spill screaming kids into the yard. I push through waist-high crowds and find Micha. Relief stretches a grin across my face, which becomes wider when Micha rushes up to me and jumps into my arms.

"Dylan," he yells. "When are you coming back to the house?"

None of us ever says *home.* You have to live somewhere more than a few months to make it feel like *home.*

"I miss you," he says accusingly. He climbs down from my arms. "Why don't you come back?"

"Ask Mom that," I say.

"Are you having a good time?" He grabs my sleeping bag. "Are you camping?"

A good time? I'm filthy, cold, and hungry. I disentangle his fingers from the sleeping bag. "Get your grimy paws off that," I say.

"Can I come camping with you?"

"Maybe in the summer," I tell him. "Are you being good in school?"

"Very good," he says, but his eyes slide away from mine.

I give him the once-over. His hair is long, falling into his eyes, but he doesn't appear any dirtier than the other kids. That makes me suspicious.

"Do we have a new dad?" I ask.

Micha shakes his head. "Not yet. After he marries Mom, Dan says he'll be my dad."

Marries? That would explain why Micha looks halfway decent. To impress Dan. Shit, he must have bought the

Italian blood story. She won't want me back, then. Not if Dan is there.

"Hey, Dylan." Jordan comes up, a small gang of boys trailing behind him.

"Hey, yourself," I say. I look hard at the boys and don't like what I see. These are the kids you find in the principal's office, in the "time-out" room, in trouble.

I grab Jordan's collar and take Micha's hand and pull them to the side of the playground. I reach into my pocket and take out a package of jelly beans and hand it to Micha. He crows his delight and tears into it. I pull another package out and hold it toward Jordan. As his hand reaches for it, I grab his wrist. "I have people watching you," I say. "All the time. You smoke, steal, mouth off at a teacher, and you'll have to answer to me."

He twists his arm from my hand and grabs the candy packet. "No you don't," he says. But his eyes are uncertain and I know he'll watch his step. For now.

Micha fishes in my pocket and brings out a handful of caramels.

"You aren't allowed on school property." A woman stands in front of me, a small kid dangling from each hand. "I'm a teacher here. What are you giving those children?"

I'm dying to tell her "Crack," but that'll just get me into trouble.

"I'm their brother," I say. "It's candy."

"Did you check in with the office first?" she asks.

"No."

"You'll have to do that or leave school property."

Stupid rule.

"I have to go, guys," I say.

Micha grabs my arm. "Stay," he pleads.

"I'll be back," I assure him. "You be good." I turn to Jordan. "Remember, I know what you're doing all the time."

I walk across the yard.

"Dylan!"

Micha's wail follows me as I go through the school gate, but I don't look back.

Chapter 6

I put my pack at my feet, loop the strap around my ankle, and settle into a chair in the reading lounge at the library. There is a small bubble of excitement in my stomach. This morning, I saw a sign in the window of a coffee shop asking for part-time help. I went in and the waitress told me to come back in the afternoon at two o'clock, when the manager would be there. This is the closest I've ever been to getting a job.

Last night was pretty much the worst I've spent since I've been on the streets. Huddled in a doorway, I kept hearing Micha cry my name over and over. But this morning, I turned around and there was the Help Wanted sign. Right over my head! With a job, I could get my own place, and Micha and Jordan could visit me. As I sit there spinning fantasies, I flip over the book I picked up on my way to the lounge, and my mouth drops open. It's the Einstein book. I study his picture. How did he ever get a job with hair like that?

I leave the book open on my lap and run over my plans. I'll sit here until one o'clock, then I'll go to the washroom and have a good wash, particularly under the arms. I've run out of deodorant and I'm fairly ripe, but if I don't get too close to the manager, he might not notice. Maybe he'll be at a desk and I'll sit across from him. I picture myself at a real job interview with a desk. It would help hide my frayed pant legs and the scuffs on my boots.

It feels so good to have plans, to have to be somewhere at a specific time. Einstein had theories about time, but I doubt he ever knew how it felt to have every day run into the next until they meld together.

When I lived with Micha and Jordan, my life was ruled by time: when they came home from school, when their stomachs got hungry, when their favourite television show came on. On the street, seconds and minutes disappear and time is measured by light and dark, by relief and fear.

My eyes fall on the opened page and I grin as I read. Seems good old Albert couldn't find a job, until a friend got him one in a patent office in Switzerland. As I turn another page, I check on Twitch.

He followed me here, walking a block behind, and now he's at the fiction bookshelves, running a finger over the spines. Occasionally, he peeks at me, but he quickly averts his face when I look up. It's annoying.

I launch myself out of my chair and nearly fall flat on my face, having forgotten about the strap around my ankle. What's scary is that not one person notices my clumsiness. Am I invisible? When I'm begging for money, people sweep past like I'm not there. Maybe I really *am* not there. Goosebumps rise on my arms as a new theory occurs to me. If no one acknowledges my existence, will I cease to be? I'm getting weird. Like the Garbage Man. Heart pounding, I grab my backpack and make my way to the fiction section. Twitch shrinks against the shelves, so, obviously, *he* sees me.

"Quit doing that," I say to Twitch.

"What?" he whispers loudly.

"Walking behind me. Hiding in the books. I'm not mad at you."

"You're not?"

"No."

How can a person be mad at him? He's pathetic.

"Listen. I have a job interview at two." A new fear assails me. Am I jinxing my chances by telling my news? "I'm going to the washroom. Don't follow me."

His face falls.

"It's not because I'm mad. It's because I don't want anyone noticing me go into the bathroom," I explain. It's like I'm talking to Micha. And if it's like I'm talking to Micha, I reason, I may as well treat him like I do Micha. Promise a reward for good behaviour. "Sit down quietly until I come back and I'll let you walk to my interview with me."

It works. Twitch sits in a chair. He puts a hand on his knee to stop it jiggling, then both hand and knee bounce.

A school class comes into the library, and in the resulting confusion I slip past the Checkout desk and into the washroom. I push each stall door. Empty. Good. I don't want some creep eyeballing my chest.

I pull my shirt off, lather soap and water together, and wash the pits well. I sniff my T-shirts, pick the least scented one, and tug it over my head. That's when I notice my hair. It's matted and dirty, but I can't wash it in the sink. I wet and smooth it as best I can with my fingers, give myself one last check, and decide I'll do.

Twitch and I leave the library. Legs a blur, he walks in front, then beside me, back and forth, making me dizzy.

"It's not sex," he says out of the blue.

"What?"

"It's not sex," he says. "With Brad. It's just a way to make a quick buck, have a warm bed for the night. But it's not sex. I'm not gay."

I merely nod, hoping he'll shut up. Talk like this makes me uncomfortable, but I know what he's getting at. There's a three-block stretch downtown where the hookers and hustlers have their turfs staked out. It's a busy place after dark. Cars slowly cruise up and down checking out the girls in skirts that barely cover their asses, while others approach the boys on their stretch. It's a desperate place too: laughing, crying, arguing, and fighting. How could anyone think it's about sex?

"Have you seen Jenna?" I ask.

"No," Twitch says, slowly.

"But . . . ?" I prod him.

"Brendan's mad at her for taking off with you like that. You need to watch out."

My heart skips a beat, but before I can give it any further thought, we're at the coffee shop.

"Okay, this is it. You stay out here," I say.

"You want me to look after your bag?" Twitch asks.

I think it over but decide to take it in with me. The truth is, I don't trust him.

"That's okay," I say.

"Sure, man." Twitch shoves something into my hand. "This is for you."

It's the Einstein book from the library, the back cover and spine torn off to remove the security tape strip.

"I saw you reading it. I thought you'd like it," he says. He's jumping out of his skin, he's so excited. "That is the right book, isn't it?"

"How many *Albert Einstein: Father of the Theory of Relativity* books could there be?" I ask him.

"Yeah, really." He nods and grins, and wipes his nose with the back of a hand. "You won't say anything about . . . ?" He stares at his toes and I see Micha pleading with me.

I hold up the book. "Our secret," I say.

"No. No. I mean about—Brad."

"Oh, that. No, I won't." The kids out here are hard on each other. I've no desire to see Twitch beaten to a pulp.

"Thanks," he says.

His eyes water up and I think that he is going to grab my hand and cover it with kisses like I'm the Pope or something, so I quickly back up. "Thanks for the book. I got to go."

As I push open the door to the coffee shop, I'm enveloped in caffeine fumes. I'd have no problem staying awake in this place. I stare at rows of coffee bins. If I got the job, I'd soon know all the names of them.

"Can I help you?" a man asks.

"I'm here to see the manager about the part-time job," I say.

"That's me."

His eyes take me in from head to toe, and they miss nothing: the scuffed shoes, frayed pants, ragged hair, backpack, sleeping bag—shit, I should have left it with Twitch.

"Have you worked in a coffee shop before?" he asks.

"No, but I'm a fast learner," I reply.

Shouldn't he be interviewing me at a desk, instead of in front of these people sipping their coffees and pretending not to listen?

He fires off rapid questions. How old am I? Worked anywhere before?

"I'm available all hours, even at night," I tell him. Warning bells immediately go off in my brain. Wrong answer.

"So you're not in school right now," he says.

I can't think fast enough. I need that desk between us.

"What's your address?"

I'm stumped. My eyes wildly roam the coffee shop as if I might find the answer printed on the chalkboard with the listing of desserts. That's when I see the computer geek from the office tower sitting at a table near the window.

The manager leaves to wait on a customer. I'm so stupid. I should have just rattled off a fake number and street name. My shoulders droop. I'm not getting the job.

The manager returns and sets a coffee on the counter. "Come back when you have a permanent address and you've cleaned yourself up." He nods at the cup. "On the house."

I want to tell him what I think of his stinking shop of flavoured beans. Tell him to shove his cup of coffee. But my hand reaches out and picks up the cup. As I turn to leave, I see Vulture sitting in a corner. He dabs at his mouth with a napkin and smiles at me. He's overhead everything. Predator eyes follow me out of the shop.

Chapter 7

I don't know why I always let myself get so excited. I should have known my mother was not going to make a new start. I should have known each new school was going to be tough. And I should definitely have known I wouldn't get that job. That's it. I refuse to have any more expectations.

I'm sitting in front of the office tower waiting for the church bells to toll the noon hour. Wind throws hard, hurting pellets of snow into my face. People will pull up their coat collars and rush right by me to the warmth of a restaurant or store. They won't want to linger and search for change. It'll be worse when the cold months of January and February strike.

The sidewalk in front of Holy Rosary Cathedral is empty. It's been that way for a couple of days, and I worry about Jenna.

I stick my feet into the sleeping bag and pull it over my knees. As I tuck the flap between my butt and the cold cement wall, a photograph falls to the ground. I snatch it up before the wind catches it.

It's my grandparents' wedding picture, in black and white, though it would be truer to say in shades of grey. The photograph reminds me of early morning. Like this picture, dawn is the time before colour comes into the world, when there's a magical play of light and dark: nuance, subtlety, gradations, and shadows. The entire texture of the city is different at dawn, softer.

I took this photograph from my grandma's dresser drawer one day. I guess that's stealing, but I needed it. I only steal things I need. In the photograph, my grandparents smile shyly. Blossom-laden branches stretch over their heads, so I know it is spring. Shadows are short, so it must be around noon, when the sun is highest. The day must be warm because a woman in the background holds a paper to her face, like a fan, and the man beside her has a jacket folded over his arm. I want to be there, in that picture. I want to feel sun warm my skin, soft wind pass through my hair, hear laughter and talk, smell the mingled perfumes of women and apple blossoms.

I have pictures of Micha and Jordan with me in a small album, one of the few items I grabbed as Mom pushed me out the door. There's a picture of her, too. I ripped a corner of it one day, planning to tear the whole thing into bits. But in the end I didn't. Once you do something, it can't be undone. Granddad told me that.

I tuck the photograph between the pages of the Einstein book, a proper place for it, I believe, since photographs are all about time. Frozen time. Somewhere I'll always be three, five, and six.

Suddenly, the book is snatched out of my hand. Startled, I look up to see Vulture leafing through the pages. "So you're the brainy type," he says.

I grab it back, and now it's Vulture who's startled. Not too many people cross him. But he lets it go. He sits on the wall beside me and casually crosses one leg over the other.

"I could use someone with brains working for me," he says.

"I'm not looking for a job."

"So that's why you left the coffee shop with your tail between your legs?" He smirks.

I feel heat rise in my face.

"It's only going to get worse out here," he continues. "The weather. And people get nastier the colder it gets. You haven't been here long enough to see that. I have. It can get real bad."

I give an involuntary shiver.

"Work for me and you'll have steady money coming in, food, a warm place to sleep."

It's tempting. I will admit it's tempting, but . . . "I'll do fine," I say.

"Out here? In the winter?" Vulture laughs unpleasantly. "All those nickels and dimes will dry up. You'll freeze your ass off, if you don't die first."

I glance over at the church.

"Oh, she'll be there," Vulture says with complete certainty, as he follows my gaze.

"Why? You just said there wasn't any money to be made out here when it's cold."

"There isn't," he agrees. "Jenna's in . . ." He stops and thinks a moment, then smiles. "Training."

I don't think I've hated anyone as much as I hate him right now. Not even Pete when he was hitting me. He was ignorant. What Vulture is doing is deliberate.

"I'm not working for you. Now or ever," I tell him.

Vulture gets up and brushes off his pants. "You'll be begging me for a job before the month is up." He points across the street to where Jenna has arrived. "See? Right on time. She does what I say. A word of warning." Vulture leans in close and stabs my chest with a finger. "She's mine. You stay away from her, and anyone and anything else that's mine, or you'll get hurt." He jabs me a second time, then saunters away as the bells strike twelve. My fists clench in helpless fury.

As I expected, most people scurry by, intent on spending as little time as possible in the miserable weather. I still ask for money, but I get nothing.

"Cold today." The computer geek holds out a steaming sausage to me. He gestures to the cart. "He's packing it in for the season. Thought you'd like one last grill."

I feel like a dog being tamed with tidbits of food, but I take the warm bun without comment. It might be all I eat today.

He sits beside me on the wall, so close his thigh nearly touches mine. I immediately move away. I knew there was a price. Tame dog.

"I don't do that," I say, voice wrapped around the sausage.

"Do what?"

"What you want." Do I have to spell it out for him? Shit, he just about sat on me.

"I don't know what you're talking about." He shakes his head, perplexed.

Is he for real?

"Sex. I don't have sex with guys. I don't care what you pay." I might have no expectations any more, but I still have standards. My body is mine.

His eyes widen at my words, then a small smile parts his lips. "Well, that's good," he says. "Because neither do I. Have sex with guys. Or pay for it," he adds.

"Oh." I lick the last trace of onion from my fingers. What does he want, then?

"My name's Glen."

He holds out his hand. I give it a brief shake.

"What's your name?" he asks.

I hesitate, then, "Dylan."

He stands. "I'm sorry you didn't get the job at the coffee shop, Dylan. Keep trying."

I stay a while longer, begging for money, and finally a fourth person I ask reaches into his pocket and dumps a handful of change into my palm. Once I get it sorted, I see it's enough to buy me a burger and fries and a hot drink to keep me through the night at Mandy's.

"Hi, Dylan." Jenna comes up, head tucked into her chest, hands thrust into her pockets for warmth. She's pasty-faced, and her eyes are red-rimmed, but whether from cold or tears or tiredness I'm not sure. Niggling at the back of my brain is Vulture's warning, but hey, she came to see me.

"Miserable day."

I spread out my sleeping bag so she can sit beside me.

"How are your brothers?"

"Doing okay. My mom's getting married."

"Another father," she says.

"Yeah. I hear Brendan isn't too happy with you."

She grimaces. "No. He isn't. Doesn't want me taking off like that any more. He says it's because he worries about me." She reaches up and pushes her hair back, and I see a yellowing bruise on her temple.

"Did he do that?"

She lets the hair fall back down. "It was my fault," she says. "I made him mad."

I snort my disbelief.

She looks away from me, embarrassed. "I'm freezing, sitting on that pavement, and I made shit. Then Brendan took it all." She begins to cry. "I have no money and I need . . . I need feminine things, you know?"

Feminine things? This sudden delicacy takes me aback. I've heard her swear with the best of them out here. I give her some of my change. "Get yourself a hot chocolate, with milk. It's better for you. I'll meet you at the donut shop in a couple hours," I tell her.

She nods listlessly and wanders away. And I, the white knight, her rescuer, head in the opposite direction to find— feminine things? I've been meaning to get some soap and deodorant anyway, so what's a few more items.

Rather than rip off the stores downtown where they'd recognize me, I walk steadily for half an hour and come across a pharmacy in a strip mall. Red and green Christmas lights are strung across windows frosted with fake snow. Inside, I grab a shopping basket, pull my hood up over my head, then, deciding that looks too suspicious, push it off again. Face tilted to the floor, I go down an aisle, hoping no one has had the bright idea to install surveillance cameras underfoot. I'm used to stealing, done it most of my life, but still my heart beats rapidly. I won't take a CD or watch or something I just want. I can live with wanting. But I can't live with needing. I grab a bar of soap and slip it into a pocket in my coat, followed by a deodorant stick. I throw a couple items in the basket so I look legit. Now for Jenna's stuff.

Following the signs suspended from the ceiling, I find the Feminine Products aisle. I stop, dismayed by the wall of merchandise in front of me. Light days, heavy days, tampons, napkins, wings . . . *wings*? It's like a secret female language! I have no idea what Jenna would use. I hear giggling behind me and whirl about to see two girls grinning at me— a male in the female aisle. My face reddens. I walk farther down the aisle, my mind frantically trying to decipher the feminine code. The girls' laughter reaches hysterical pitch. I

focus my eyes and discover I'm in front of the condom display. At the moment, I have no need of them, but pride
makes me take a pack anyway. As I barrel up the female aisle,
I reach out a hand and grab the first package I touch. It'll
have to do. Face burning, I drop the basket, while deftly
shoving the stolen items into my coat pockets. I walk rapidly
through the security scanner, breaking into a run as a siren
shrieks. Dodging people, across a street, dodging cars, down
an alleyway, dodging drunks, through a second alley that
exits onto a crowded street. Here, I stop running and match
the pace of the people around me. Adrenaline thrums loudly
in my ears. Exhausted, I lean against a wall and close my
eyes, breathing hard.

"Hey, you!"

My eyes fly open. Cops. Two of them. It flits through my
brain how embarrassing it will be to be caught with condoms
and feminine products. Take that to court and even the
judge will snicker.

"Have you seen this girl?" One officer holds out a picture.
Jenna stares back at me.

"No."

"You sure?"

"Yeah." I look the cop directly in the eyes.

"Well, let us know if you do. She's a runaway. Her parents
are looking for her." He tucks the picture back into his
pocket. "She's fourteen."

"Fourteen?" I blurt out in my surprise.

"Yeah. They get younger all the time."

Jenna said she was nearly sixteen. Well, it's up to her if she
wants to go home or not. If she doesn't want to, then I'll take
care of her, me, the white knight with the feminine products.

"You better move along," the second officer says. "I don't

think this guy wants you propping up his wall." He points to a grim-faced man standing in the window of the store behind me.

They step back and I walk away. They know I'm living on the streets, but they're not concerned. They don't have a picture of me to flash around.

With a couple blocks behind me, I start to relax. I think about Jenna being grateful when I show her what I've got. But I'm not the white knight, I decide. I'm more like Robin Hood, taking from the rich and giving to the poor. And the stores are rich. Packed to the ceiling with Christmas merchandise. When you see that much stuff out there, you've got to think some of it's for you. But Robin Hood only takes what is needed. Jenna can be my Maid Marian.

I walk into the warmth of Mandy's and stop short. Jenna is there, but she is sitting with Vulture and a girl whose back is to me. Slowly, I make my way to the table.

"Oh, Dylan," Jenna says happily. "We were just talking about you. Brendan says it's nice the way you've been keeping an eye on me."

Yeah, right. Vulture's eyes lock with mine, and they're not *nice*.

"Anyway, it was just a misunderstanding between us, and everything's better now. We're all friends again." She beams her one-hundred-watt smile around the table.

"Oh, this is Amber." Jenna waves a hand at the girl.

"We know each other." Amber grins hugely. She waves a hand with a cigarette in it toward me.

If I'd known Amber was sitting there, I would have left immediately. When I first saw her, it was my second night on the streets, a rain-soaked, miserable night. She was leaning into a car window, negotiating with a trick, though I didn't know that at the time. Suddenly, she leapt back and the car sped away into the night, tires spinning on a wet street. She saw me watching and laughed. "You win some, you lose some," she said.

Well, what she really said was, "You fucking win some, you fucking lose some." Amber is tall, nearly as tall as me, with golden skin and black hair bound into countless tiny braids. From a distance, she looks amazing. Up close, you see the acne scars, the nicotine-stained teeth and drug-hollow eyes. Every sentence out of her mouth is *effing* this or *effing* that. Sometimes out here, people swear to prove they're not scared. You can't ever show you're scared, even if you are. It makes you vulnerable. But Amber curses like it's a natural part of the English language.

"Yep, we fucking know each other," Amber repeats.

My cheeks turn hot. We do it one time and she thinks she *knows* me. She had a rented room, filthy, but it was somewhere to sleep in relative safety. I stayed with her for a week. It was Amber who showed me how to beg for money, how to avoid cops, punks, told me the rules of the street, and one night we slept together. "You know, most people pay fucking good money for what you're getting for free," she said to me. That totally grossed me out. Next morning, I left while she slept. I'm not sure if I'm ashamed of her, or me, so it's just easier to avoid her.

"Oh, that's great," Jenna says. "You're friends."

She's bouncing on the seat, totally oblivious to the undercurrents all around her. Naive or—I look at her more closely—stoned. Definitely, stoned.

"Seems Dylan has a lot of friends," Vulture puts in. He lights a cigarette, takes a drag, and lets loose a long stream of smoke. "A man can't have too many friends."

"And," Jenna breaks in, "Brendan's given me a nickname. Jewel. We should give Dylan a nickname." She's talking so fast, the words tumble over each other. Must be some kind of pick-me-up Vulture gave her.

"Sure," Vulture says. "What do you think? Stringbean?"

Amber shoots a troubled glance from Vulture to me. She stubs her cigarette out in an ashtray.

"No, thanks," I say.

"But everyone has a nickname," Jenna says.

"Come on. Don't be such an asshole. Make the girl happy. Let her pick a name for you," Vulture says.

"I don't want a name." You get a street name and it means you belong here. They're your family and you're one of them. I'm not one of them and I do not want a nickname that says I am.

I leave, preferring the cold and snow to Vulture's company. I stop at the first trash bin I find and dump the feminine products.

Chapter 8

"In summer, it's a big street party every Friday and Saturday night down here," Twitch says. "The burbie kids come slumming. It's great. Too bad you weren't around then."

Twitch was around then. He is eighteen and he's been on the street for four years.

There's not much partying going on in early December. We're too busy trying to stay warm and worrying about the really cold months ahead.

We're at the youth centre. The first time I've been. It was Twitch who wanted to come today. Nagged me about it so much I finally agreed just to shut him up.

A checkerboard, red and black squares and pieces, is set up between us, though the play is slow. Twitch can't grasp the concept of the game. He coughs, catches his breath, then bends in a second spasm of coughing. His hacking is echoed throughout the centre. There's a lot of flu around.

He fishes in his pocket, pulls out a cigarette package and lighter. I want to tell him those won't help his health, but say instead, "Your move. Red's mine," I add, as his hand hovers over my player.

Feet beating a non-stop dance beneath the table, he leans forward and examines the board, then pulls back, only to repeat the movement again. It wears me out to watch him, so I look around the room.

It used to be an old store, with puke-green walls and a worn linoleum floor. The landlord can't rent it in this condition, so he generously lets it be used as a youth centre—for a tax break. I tip my chair back to see the ceiling, but it is obscured by a thin layer of blue smoke. Everybody smokes here but me.

Half a dozen tables are scattered about the room, surrounded by a motley collection of chairs in various states of repair. Only a few are occupied, but, to my annoyance, Amber is seated in one of them, mouth motoring, laugh scraping on my nerves. She's dressed in a skimpy skirt, high heels with no stockings, and a tight sweater—her working clothes. A sudden image of Jenna in the same outfit leaves me feeling ill.

An extra loud burst of laughter from her makes me wince. Twitch looks up, catches my eye, and grimaces. He's not all that bad, Twitch.

A man and two women staff the centre. Originally, I thought they'd be preaching to us, but to my surprise they leave us alone. There's a pot of soup on a small table against one wall, bowls, and a basket of sandwiches beside it that you can help yourself to. I did. A can sits beside the food in case you have money to make a donation toward the centre. It's empty.

A bulletin board by the soup has flyers pinned on it about the dangers of AIDS, drugs, and alcohol, also counselling services and dates and times a street nurse is available.

Twitch finally moves his black piece, smiles broadly, and sits back. I immediately jump his man and add it to the growing pile of his players I've collected.

"Shit." He blows a stream of smoke away to the side, leans forward, and studies the board, fingers reaching, drawing back, writhing together. I wonder if he was always this way or if it's the drugs killing his brain cells. I settle in for a long game.

One of the staff, a gaunt woman with a cap of black, curly hair and dark eyes, goes around the room handing out a flyer. She slaps one on our table. Close up, I see that she is younger than I first thought. Mid-twenties, I guess. I also see the old tracks from needles that run up her arm into the sleeve of her T-shirt. "You boys might be interested in this," she says. "If you have any questions, just ask."

I pick up the flyer. It's about an alternative school for street kids. The word *computers* catches my interest momentarily, but I let it go. I push the flyer in front of Twitch.

"So who has time for that?" I say.

He glances briefly at the flyer, then back to the checker-board. "Yeah, who?"

I start to wad it into a ball, then quickly fold it and push it into my pack. You never know when a piece of paper might come in handy.

A hand falls on my shoulder. Startled, I swing around to see Amber.

"Whoa." She takes a step back and holds up her hands in front of herself. "It's just me. Remember?"

"I know who you are," I say testily.

She falls into a chair, legs askew. Not a pretty sight with that short skirt. I think how much more gracefully Jenna would have sat.

"I thought perhaps you'd fucking forgotten. I don't see you around any more," she says.

"I've been busy," I tell her. "You know."

The braids are gone today, and her hair hangs in strings in her eyes. It needs a good wash. In fact, she needs a good wash. But then, who am I to talk?

"How you doing, Twitch?" she asks.

"Good," he says.

"Can I bum a cigarette?"

Twitch reaches into his coat pocket and pulls out a package of cigarettes and hands it to her. "One," he cautions, "and I'm watching you, so don't try to take any more."

"So how's Jenna these days?" I ask. I reach into my bag and pull out the Einstein book to show it's just a casual question.

"Not much changed from last week," Amber says shortly. "You got the fucking hots for her or something?"

I don't bother to answer.

She flicks ash in the general direction of a cup. "I wouldn't go around broadcasting that. Good way to get your fucking head bashed in," Amber says. "She's Brendan's property."

"Yeah? Well, you're Brendan's *property*, too," I say nastily.

She glares at me. "So? At least I have money. My own place."

"That dump?"

"I didn't hear you complaining when you needed a place to stay," she says.

I'm tired of the conversation, so I flip open the book and pretend to read. Amber leans forward and spreads her fingers over the page in front of me, covering the words. "You just fucking leave? You don't say goodbye? You get up in the morning and fucking leave? That's no way to treat a friend." She gets to her feet. "See you around, Twitch." She wanders across the room.

"She's pissed at you," Twitch says.

"I didn't do anything," I protest. "I stayed with her a few

days when I first got here, then I left. Big deal. She's putting on weight," I add.

"She's pregnant." Twitch moves a checker piece and sits back, smiling smugly.

"Pregnant?" My heart skips a beat. "How pregnant?"

"I dunno," Twitch says. "About five months, I guess."

Well, that lets me off the hook. But a baby. Out here? It's none of my business. Every man—and woman—for themselves. I jump Twitch's piece.

"Hey, you know who the two smartest guys in the world were?" I ask Twitch.

He's studying the board, so I go on.

"Isaac Newton and Albert Einstein. Einstein taught himself physics." Who needs school? "Read this." I push the book over to Twitch.

He waves it away. "I'm concentrating, man. You read it."

I pull the book back in front of me. *We live in a quantum universe, one built out of tiny, discrete chunks of energy and matter,*" I read. "Hey, we're just little bits of energy and matter, Twitch."

A cloud of acrid smoke is blown in my face. But it's not from Twitch. A chair is pulled out from our table and a body plops into it. Uninvited.

"What's happening?" A smoky inquiry.

I look the newcomer over before answering. Early twenties, big guy, as tall as me, but bulky to go with it. The chair creaks beneath his weight. He pulls his coat off and sets it over the back of the chair, and I see biceps strain against black T-shirt sleeves. The shirt looks a size too small, worn purposely that way to set his muscles off. Light bounces off a freshly shaven pink scalp.

"Not much," I say shortly. I don't want to be friendly, and

yet—I take in the skull-and-crossbones tattoo stretching up his neck—I don't want to be unfriendly, either.

"He's beating you bad, Twitch." The cigarette gestures toward my pile of captured pieces, scattering ash over the board.

I glance at Twitch, surprised that he knows the man, but he's avoiding my eyes. His leg is beating a fast staccato beneath the table. Real nervous, even for Twitch. I get a bad feeling.

"Who's your friend, Twitch?"

"Dylan, Lurch. Lurch, Dylan."

Lurch? I swallow a snicker. What the hell kind of name is Lurch? I steal another look at him. I guess it's the kind of name you can have if you're that big and that menacing.

"You ever been inside?" Lurch asks.

"Inside where?" I ask.

"Inside. Jail. Prison."

I shake my head.

"I've been in and out of detention centres and jails all my life," Lurch says. "Break and enter, assault, auto theft."

I don't get why he's telling me this.

Lurch drops his cigarette butt on the floor and grinds it with the heel of a black army boot. He immediately lights another one. He stabs a finger at Twitch. "I bet you've been inside."

Twitch jerks, but presses his lips together and says nothing.

"I bet they took you apart in there." Lurch laughs.

Twitch leaps to his feet, sending his chair flying over backward with a bang. The place jumps. Everyone is suddenly alert. The staff spread out across the room.

"I'm going to the can," Twitch mutters.

Behind him, Amber sidles toward the door.

"I see you, little girl," Lurch calls. "Aren't you supposed to be working?" A sharp *crack* as he slaps his hand down on the table, and Amber bolts out the door. That's when I realize who he is. Vulture's henchman.

"Just the two of us," Lurch says. He grins widely and I see a gap in his bottom teeth where one is missing. He swings his chair around to face me and straddles it. Adrenaline races through my body—fight or flight. I strip the board of the playing pieces, willing my hands not to shake.

"Want to take me on?"

Fear stops my heart, but Lurch points at the board.

"No," I say.

"Good decision. Last person who lost to me is still looking for his teeth."

What's he trying to do? Prove he's the baddest of the bad?

"Don't say much, do you?"

I shrug, and let him interpret that any way he wants.

"How long you been living on the street?" Lurch asks.

I examine the question from all sides but see no reason not to answer. "About six weeks," I say.

"Mom and Dad throw you out?"

I start, but it's a stab in the dark. He couldn't know. I lean down and stuff the Einstein book in my pack and fasten the straps.

"Rough living on the street." Lurch butts out the second cigarette, takes out a pack, and offers one to me. I shake my head.

"Don't smoke? Smart. You'll live longer." Somehow he makes it sound like a threat. "Listen, I can help you make some easy money."

"I'm not interested," I say. It'll be drugs or sex or stealing.

"You haven't even heard what I've to offer," Lurch continues, with an injured air. "You could have a nice apartment of your own, good food. The streets are a dangerous place. A person could get hurt all on his own."

The black-haired woman comes up with a cloth and wipes the table beside us. Lurch sends her a dirty look, but she just keeps giving the table the best clean it's had in a long time.

The door to the centre opens and the Garbage Man steps inside and stops. He's too old for this place, so I'm surprised when the woman greets him warmly. He stands in the doorway, eyes darting everywhere, until they land on Lurch. He takes a step backward, but the woman beckons him into the room. After a moment, garbage-bagged feet swish past us. Arms poke through holes in a second bag, and a third is pulled over his head and ears and fastened with twine that disappears into a bushy beard. His attire is apt because the Garbage Man is a dumpster diver—a person who gets his meals out of the trash bins behind restaurants.

He hugs the outside of the room as he makes his way to the soup pot. Lurch suddenly leaps up, and growls. Alarmed, the man scuttles backward, flips over a chair, and falls flat on his ass.

"You can leave." The woman locks eyes with Lurch.

I have to admire the way she stands there, dwarfed by this guy and armed only with a dirty dishrag.

Lurch laughs and pulls on his coat. "Think over what I said," he tells me.

"I'm not interested," I say. "And you can tell Brendan that."

I don't know why I added that last bit. I could have just nodded and tried to keep out of Lurch's way for the rest of my life. Maybe it was the woman standing up to him that made me do it.

His face clouds over. "You might become interested," he says, voice hard. "Tell Twitch I got a gift for him. He knows where he can find me."

He pulls the door open, and the pamphlets on the bulletin board flutter in the draft as he leaves.

"You're in trouble. You're going to have to watch yourself all the time." Twitch has resurfaced from the bathroom.

"I do that anyway," I say, nonchalant, though my insides wobble alarmingly. "He says he has a gift for you."

Twitch's eyes light up, and I know the gift is a hit. He rapidly pulls on his long black overcoat, and suddenly, the pieces all fall together. A gift. It was Twitch who insisted we to go the centre today. I'm so stupid. There are no real friends on the street. You've got to look out for yourself. That's not a theory. It's just the way it is.

Chapter 9

I've decided to keep a low profile for a couple of days. The popular theory is that a person should stand up to bullies like Lurch and Vulture, but mine is that a person should keep his own teeth for as long as possible.

I'm sitting on the wall outside the office tower waiting for the lunch crowd. Low profile or not, I need money to eat. Lemon yellow sun seeps into the ancient brick of the church, turning it golden. Another beam melts yesterday's patches of snow on the sidewalk. I unzip my coat and raise my face to the sky. As I do, I'm reminded of a textbook picture I once saw, of ancient priests in the middle of their ceremonies, faces raised to the sun. They knew that was where the real power lay. Einstein knew it, too. I can see him, head tilted back like my own, brow furrowed as he contemplated the sun and the universe beyond.

"Hey, Dylan." Jenna—I refuse to call her Jewel—sits on the wall beside me.

My heart skips a sickening beat, and I can't stop myself searching nervously for Vulture.

"Great day, isn't it?" she says, but her voice lacks animation. "I was totally wasted last night."

Her hair still gleams, but there are purple smudges beneath her eyes and her chin has sprouted a cluster of angry-looking pimples. There is also, I see, a second bruise on her temple, almost on top of the old yellowing one.

The church bell rings the noon hour.

"Oh, shit. Is it that late? I better get going." She darts across the street to the church and sits on the sidewalk. Behind her is an activity board with a sign announcing a hospitality dinner tonight. Free food for the poor people.

The twelfth chime fades and I count the people coming from the tower doors. One, two, three—the fourth person tosses me a loonie. After that, it's a flood. I don't bother to count. First, second, or third—the warm weather is making them all generous. For ten minutes I'm busy, then the crowds thin. I carefully stack the pile of coins on the wall beside me and add it up: fourteen dollars and thirty-five cents. I scoop the change into my coat pocket as Glen, the computer geek, comes up to me.

"I thought you might be able to use these." He holds out a pair of gloves and a wool toque with a dorky tassel on the end.

The feeling of being tamed hits me again, so I don't take them. Finally, he sets them on the wall, then sits on the other side of them, far away from me. "You won't need them today," he says. "This is a great bit of weather we're being treated to. It won't last, though."

He's right. I take out the Einstein book, place it on the wall, and shove the gloves into my backpack, followed by the toque. "Thanks."

Glen picks up the book. "So you're reading about Albert Einstein," he says. He fingers the torn spine.

"It was a gift," I say quickly.

"From the library?"

"I didn't steal it," I insist.

He leafs through the pages, stopping at the photograph of Einstein. "He's a strange-looking one, isn't he? But then, I think a lot of geniuses are odd-looking."

"If that's your theory," I say, "then most of the people walking around down here are geniuses." Downtown has more than its fair share of strange. It's like someone ordained that all the weird people on the planet had to live within these few city blocks. "Like her."

I point at the Swear Lady, a gypsy of the streets. Dressed in tattered layers of skirts and tops and shawls, she could be thirty or a hundred. All her belongings are stacked in a shopping cart that she guards with her life. As she walks, she litters the air with shouted obscenities. She passes us, whips around, and lets loose a stream of filth at Glen before moving on.

He grins. "Yeah, I see your point."

A sheet of paper floats out of the book. Glen bends to pick it up from the ground and turns it over. It's the flyer from the youth centre. "Are you thinking of going back to school?" he asks.

I don't answer.

"It'd be a good idea if you did," he goes on.

I slowly run my eyes over his expensive leather bomber jacket, the casual pants and sweater that probably cost the world. He has the grace to flush.

"I know you don't have money to go to school. I only meant that this is a good way to get an education. I know this place. I help out there on weekends, though my role is for support purposes only. You can study at your own speed. You don't have to deal with discipline, or rules, or teachers, and you can have a peer tutor, someone your age," he says eagerly.

I wish he'd shut up about his stupid school. It takes all my time just to stay alive. There's none left over for studying. I snatch the paper from him, crush it in my fist, and let it drop to the ground.

He flushes again, in anger this time, but he speaks lightly. "Didn't your mother ever teach you not to litter?"

He scoops the paper up, smooths it out on his knee, and places it in the Einstein book. He hands the book to me. I carelessly shove it into my backpack.

"My mother never taught me anything," I tell him. "She didn't have time. She had three kids to take care of."

It's a lie. That's what she should have done, but it's what I did. But Glen doesn't need to know that.

"I'm sorry," he says. "It sounds like you've had a difficult time."

His apology unnerves me.

"So, do you have sisters or brothers or one of each?"

He obviously doesn't know the rules, but then he doesn't live on the street.

"Brothers. They're younger than me." Suddenly, my eyes swim with tears. I look away from him, terrified I'll blubber all over the place. "Jordan's ten, Micha's six," I say. More information than I normally give, but I need time to get myself under control.

He stands up. "I have to get back to the office. It's been nice talking to you."

I watch the leather jacket go through the tower doors and

out of view. I should stop coming to this spot. There must be all kinds of places I can hustle for money. I don't need preachy crap from someone like Glen. I decide then and there that I'm not coming back—after the lunch crowd returns. They must be good for at least a few more coins.

Jenna darts across the street from the church. "How are you doing?"

"Okay," I say shortly. I'm still nursing my anger.

"I'm making a killing." She shakes the basket and I hear the clink of coins.

"Vulture will be happy," I say unkindly.

"Vulture?"

"That's what I call Brendan. It's the nickname that I made up for him."

"Why Vulture?" she asks.

"Think about it," I say. "Are you going to get any of that money?"

Her face crumples and I feel like a total creep.

"There's a hospitality dinner at the church tonight. Free meal. Do you want to go?" This is as close to an apology as I can offer.

She tosses her silver hair and smiles widely. "Sure. Meet you here at six." She waves, and takes off down the street. I'm amazed I have a date.

Busy with the returning work crowd, I don't notice the four punks approach. Then suddenly, they're here, in my face. People give us a wide berth, feeling the menace in the air. I slowly tuck my backpack behind me.

One sits beside me, while three others stand in a semi-circle in front. All wear red bandanas on their heads, military boots on their feet.

The one sitting is my age, his face a festering mass of nasty-looking pimples.

"You do good here?" He gestures to the office tower.

A metal stud in his tongue. I give a mental shudder, but don't answer.

"Looks like a good place, don't it?" he says to the others. One nods. "Profitable," he continues. He wipes his nose on the sleeve of an old army jacket, then spits.

Fear is a rushing sound, like water, in my ears.

"I just decided. This is our turf now," the kid says.

He shoves me sideways, and my hand grapples for my pack.

"Don't come back."

I had already decided to leave, but now that they want my spot—I'm keeping it. I don't get up from the wall. "It's a free country. I'll go where I want."

"What are you? Stupid?" The Bandana Kid gets to his feet. The others crowd closer, looming over me. I hear a click. See a glint of silver blade. I imagine it plunged into me. The cut. The blood. The pain.

"Cops," a girl's voice warns.

And they melt away into the concrete city. Only Twitch and Amber are left. I'm not sure when they arrived, but Amber saved my ass. I don't particularly like that thought, because I can see she knows it, too. She sits beside me and lights up a cigarette. For once, I wish I smoked. Sweat runs down my back and my legs shake.

"You really don't know when to fucking leave it alone," Amber says.

Twitch hops up and down in front of us. "You could have been killed, man."

I shrug, trying to show a cool I don't feel.

"Where's the cop?" I ask Amber.

"That security guard there." She points her cigarette toward the office building.

"A security guard?"

"It's a fucking uniform. It got rid of them, didn't it?"

"I guess," I say.

"Well, you're very welcome," she says.

"It's not good to smoke when you're pregnant."

"I'm cutting back," she replies, unperturbed.

"It's really bad for the baby," I go on. What the hell's the matter with me?

"I fucking know that," Amber says, beginning to get annoyed.

"Okay, I was just saying, that's all."

"You're a fucking ungrateful jerk. Gotta go to work." She stubs out the half-smoked cigarette, tucks it into her pocket for later, and strolls away. "Try not to get yourself killed," she calls back. "I can't always be around."

"Hey, Twitch," I say. "Jenna and I are going to the hospitality dinner tonight at the church." I nod toward Holy Rosary Cathedral. "You want to come?" Relieved that I'm not a grease spot on the ground, I forget that I'm not having anything to do with him any more.

"With Jenna?" Twitch shrieks. "You got a death wish?"

I hoist my pack onto my back. "I need a bathroom. Come on. I'll buy you some fries at Mandy's."

"You have money?" Twitch says, hopefully. He wants a hit. I've seen Twitch get down and lick the sidewalk after a cocaine deal just in case some was spilled.

"I'm only offering fries," I tell him.

Twitch unfolds himself from the wall, long and skinny. "I

may as well take you up on that offer while I can," he says. "I won't get fries from a dead man."

I grin like I don't care, but as we head to the donut shop, the sound of the metallic click plays over and over in my mind.

Chapter 10

Mist clings to the trees and hangs in orange shrouds from the street lights. A bus swishes past, tires singing on the wet pavement. As I wait for Jenna and Twitch in front of the church, I read the announcements: *Advent Sunday, Evening Mass Saturday at 5:00.*

The Swear Lady arrives at the bottom of the stone steps of the church with her shopping cart. Cursing fiercely, she struggles to lift it up, but the step is too narrow and the wheels slip back down. She kicks the metal side and swears in frustration. She wants that meal, but her life is in that shopping cart and she is not leaving it behind. Unceasing obscenities flow from her mouth as she goes to the front of the cart and hauls it up, step by step, until she reaches the top. She disappears from view with a final flap of a scarf.

The bells chime six o'clock. A soft drizzle falls on my upturned face as I study the lighted twin spires of the church. They rise above the bare branches of the trees toward heaven—or where most people assume heaven is. Gargoyles, elongated creatures with distorted animal and human features, are perched on each corner of the church and tucked beneath the eaves. They're interesting, but it's the spires I like: their symmetry and gracefulness. Holy Rosary is an old church, sitting unperturbed between two office towers, but not as old or elaborate as Europe's cathedrals. I've seen pictures of them—sweeping arches, soaring ceilings, magnificent domes and stonework—and been blown away by the mathematics and skill required to build them. I wonder how it would feel to stand in front of a church and know I created such beauty. An intense yearning swells my chest, and I don't notice Jenna beside me until she tugs on my sleeve.

"What's so interesting up there?" she asks, head tilted back to peer at the spires.

"Gargoyles," I say. "In old times, gargoyles, those carvings"—I point to one—"used to be the downspouts for buildings. There are some on the library and the older bank buildings down here, but now, they're just decoration." I sound like an amazingly boring tour guide.

"How do you know about this stuff?" Jenna asks.

"Read it somewhere, I guess. Facts seem to stick with me." Lamer and lamer.

Twitch barrels down the sidewalk, all legs and arms, and runs into me. In turn, I fall against Jenna.

"Can't you take something for that?" I say, irritably.

"For what?" Twitch asks.

"For having more arms and legs than the average person. For coordination. For . . ." I flounder, "for being *you*."

"Downers sometimes help," he says. He doubles over coughing.

"I mean real medication. From a doctor."

"You mean, like the stuff they had me on in school?" Twitch says after he catches his breath.

"Let's go in." I don't want to hear Twitch's sorry life story.

"Every lunch hour, a huge line of us kids formed up outside the office," Twitch continues.

I guess we're going to hear it anyway.

"You're a little bit hyper, a little mouthy, you know?" His hands flap wildly through the air. "The teacher complains that you're distracting the class, and boom, you find yourself in this line to get drugs to shut you up."

"Ritalin," Jenna interjects.

"Let's go in," I say.

"Wait a sec." Twitch grabs my arm. "Here's Amber."

She rushes up, out of breath.

"Who said you could come?" I demand.

"What? Is it an invitation-only party?" Amber replies.

"I did," Jenna says at the same time.

"Well, okay, I guess," I bluster.

Jenna pulls open the door and Amber follows her inside. "Fuck you," she whispers as she passes me. We go down a short flight of stairs.

"What's that stuff called again?" Twitch asks Jenna.

"Ritalin. They give it to hyperactive kids to shut them up. I've seen those lineups. They're the troublemakers," she explains.

"I never knew what it was called," Twitch says. "It made me feel strange."

"How could you tell? You're always strange," I tell him.

"Twitch, you just tell him to go fuck himself," Amber calls back.

"You can't swear in here," Jenna whispers, face shocked. "It's a church!"

I can't help wondering how the Swear Lady is getting on. Has she been struck down for blasphemy yet?

A rich scent of tomato and garlic wafts up the church steps. At the bottom of the stairs, a line snakes slowly forward. Jenna picks up a tray from a stack, hands it to Amber, and passes one back to me. Twitch reaches around me and grabs one, nearly sending the pile flying. I quickly steady it.

"Smells great," he says. I feel him moving behind me, picking at his face, shifting the tray, shuffling his feet.

And then we're in front of the food.

"Lasagna?" A woman holds out a slab of pasta.

"Sure," I say. I should thank her, but I don't want to be grateful for the food.

"What's that?" Twitch points to a bowl of lettuce and dressing.

"Caesar salad," Jenna says.

"Help yourself," the woman with the lasagna says. "And take some fruit for dessert."

I heap salad on a second plate and take an apple. After a moment's thought, I take a second one, for tomorrow's breakfast.

Twitch stares open-mouthed at the heaping bowls of salad and fruit. I know what he's going through. It's a bit of a culture shock to someone brought up on white bread and packaged macaroni and cheese to see fresh food. I toss an orange and an apple on his tray, followed by a carton of milk, then push him along so he doesn't hold up the line. Again, it's feels just like I'm taking care of Micha and Jordan. And with that thought, the tears threaten again. What the hell is going on? I catch Amber watching me.

"Lots of onions in the lasagna," I say, covering myself in case a tear rolls down my cheek.

We sit at a table, one of several set up in the church basement. Most people have chosen their seats carefully, a chair between them and their neighbour. I recognize a few of the library lounge crazies. The Garbage Man sits in his green bags across from the Swear Lady. Kids from the youth centre are clustered together at one end of a table, among them two of the Bandana Kids. I feel a spurt of alarm, but they're too busy eating to notice me. At least thirty people are in the room, but the only sounds are a baby's cries and the Swear Lady's curses. An air of exhaustion hangs over everyone, almost visible it is so strong. The thin woman from the youth centre is there, scrubbing down tables. I might have known she'd be part of a church. A do-gooder. Out to save the world and my ass. She pulls out a chair, wipes it down, then sits.

"Hello," she says cheerfully.

I know exactly where this is going. "Don't even bother," I say, as I push a fork piled with lasagna into my mouth. It tastes wonderful.

"Bother to do what?" the woman says, bewildered.

I swallow and face her. "I know I'm eating your food, but I don't believe in God, and nothing you can say is going to change that," I tell her grandly.

"It must be hard to walk around with all that weight," she says.

Now it's my turn to look puzzled.

"From the chip on here." She taps my shoulder. "I don't go to this or any other church. I'm helping out today because they're short-handed. Whether I believe in God or not, or whether you do, is our own business. Don't worry, I'm not going to convert you."

"Oh." I feel cheated. I'd been all set to get into an argument.

"I saw you at the drop-in centre. I'm Ainsley."

She sticks out her hand and her sleeve rides up to reveal a criss-cross of scars on her wrist. Suddenly, I see red blood flowing from the wounds down her hands. Life dripping from her fingers. I set my fork down on the plate, appetite gone. I'm losing my mind.

She drops her hand and pulls her sleeve down. "That was from a different time," she says. "I know Amber and Twitch . . ." She scrutinizes Jenna, and I'm reminded of the police and the photograph.

"I'm Jewel, and this is Dylan." Jenna introduces us politely, like we're at afternoon tea with the Queen. I can't believe her sometimes.

Twitch pushes his plate back, food nearly untouched, and coughs deeply.

"You don't sound too great," Ainsley says. "You need a doctor." Then she turns to me. "I like the way you stood up to that jerk at the centre the other day. That takes a lot of courage."

Courage? Try stupidity. But I don't say that out loud. Not with Jenna here.

"You shouldn't be mixing it up with Lurch," Amber says. "You're fuc—" She swallows the word with difficulty. "You're asking for trouble."

"Death wish," Twitch says.

"Shut up!" I tell both of them.

Ainsley gets up and gives the table a swipe with her cloth. "If any of you need anything, you know where to find me."

"She's nice," Jenna says, after Ainsley leaves.

It's suddenly too hot in the church hall. Police, photographs, scars on wrists. I can't think straight. My chair slides noisily across the floor as I push back from the table. "I got to go. I'll catch up with you guys later."

I leave the room and charge up the stairs, taking in great gulps of air to steady myself. At the outside doors, I stop. Wide stone stairs lead away from me into the church. Slowly, silently, I climb, feeling like I'm ascending into heaven. At the top of the stairs, heavy, carved wooden doors are closed. I gently pull on one, expecting it to be locked, but it opens effortlessly. I slip inside and the door shuts, muffling the city sounds, leaving me in a hushed space.

It takes a moment for my eyes to adjust to the gloom. Soft yellow lights glow along the walls. I'm reminded of the light I put in Micha's bedroom to ease his nightmares. Are these God's nightlights? Or would those be the moon and the stars? I breathe in the smell of God: musty books, lemon furniture polish, and a sickly sweet odour I can't identify. As I walk up an aisle, my foot knocks against a pew. The resulting bang echoes into a high ceiling that the lights don't reach. The church is big, much bigger than the plain white wooden church my grandma and granddad took me to, yet it shares the same restful silence. Maybe God gets tired of hearing our groans and moans and needs some quiet—like my mother did when she had a bad headache and we boys were fighting. *Shut up in there or I'll give you something to yell about!*

I walk up the side aisle and study the elaborately painted walls, the carved columns, the stained-glass windows and the statues set every few steps. In contrast, Grandma and Granddad's church was stark and simple. Same God, two very different churches. I wonder if He has a preference.

I stop in front of a statue of a man, hands outstretched, sculpted brown hair over his shoulders, face frozen in a bemused smile. Jesus. I remember that much from the few times I went to church. A large cross hangs on the wall behind the altar; another man is suspended from it, hands nailed to the crosspiece. Jesus again. No wonder he had that bemused smile back there. Anyone would if they knew they were going to be nailed to a cross

Then I see it, a statue of a woman with a baby on her lap, and I catch my breath. This is old, much older than the church, yet the woman's face is eternally young, born again in Jenna. It gives me the creeps how much she looks like Jenna, yet I can't look away because the statue is beautiful.

"Lovely, isn't it? Someone told me it was sent from Rome." Ainsley has come up behind me, coat on, obviously on her way out. Probably scared I'll steal the church's silver.

She examines the statue. "You know, she sort of has the look of that girl who was with you," she says. "What's her name again?"

"Jewel," I say. With the police looking for Jenna, I don't want to use her real name.

"She's young," Ainsley says. "Jewel, I mean. It scares me to death, these young girls out here. I worry what can happen to them."

"What would you know about it?"

"I was one of them," Ainsley says shortly.

She turns and walks partway down the aisle. "We shouldn't be in here."

"I thought God's house was everyone's house," I say flippantly. But a part of me is hurting. Longing. "Einstein didn't believe in God," I say suddenly. It feels safer having Einstein say it, considering where I am and the possibility of lightning bolts.

"Einstein?" Ainsley says.

"Yeah, the genius. I'm reading a book on him. He didn't believe God existed."

A smile slowly blossoms across Ainsley's face. "You read. Come on, you non-believer. We have to get out of here before someone finds us. We're supposed to stay in the basement," she says.

As I follow her down the aisle, I draw in one last breath of

God's smell and wish I could come back. It wouldn't matter whether I believed in him or not. The stained-glass windows could splash red and blue over me, I could slide my butt over the polished pews, study the paintings on the walls and ceilings and admire the statues, and maybe—belong.

Chapter 11

The Garbage Man snores softly across from me in the library lounge. He reeks with a stink radius of half the room. I sniff my own pits discreetly. How big is my stink radius?

I watch the hands of the clock on the wall race toward closing time. It's strange how, when I'm out on the street and it's freezing, time ticks with excruciating slowness, but when I want it to move slower, it speeds up. Do you have a mathematical formula for that anomaly, Einstein?

I don't have the nerve to pull out the ripped-off Einstein book here, so I'm flipping through the pages of a book on gargoyles, though mostly I'm focused on the clock. Really focused, as in obsessed. I bet that's how the Garbage Man started. Got obsessed with those green bags, and things deteriorated from there.

"Ten minutes until we close," a disembodied voice announces. "Please bring all books to the Checkout counter."

I jump to my feet and grab my pack, heading for one last pit stop at the washroom before I hit the streets. I've pretty much lived in the library the past two days. Yesterday, like the day before, I peered around the corner of the office tower to see the Bandana Kid and his friends sitting there. In my spot. Taking my money. I'll have to find a new place to beg soon, because I'm almost out of cash.

I hold the gloves Glen gave me beneath the dryer in the washroom to warm them. I wonder if he came by today and saw the Bandana Kids. Did he sit down and talk to them?

I head into the cold, my hands shoved inside the warm gloves. The temperature dropped all day and—I sniff—there is a metallic smell of approaching snow. I remember Granddad sniffing the air and telling Grandma the weather. His nose was as accurate as those jokers on television with all their Doppler radar crap.

At the bottom of the library's granite steps, I stand and look up and down the sidewalk. Which way to go? Doesn't matter. I don't know where, or if, I'll sleep tonight. I can't go to Mandy's. Despite my one moment of bravado at the church dinner, I'm leery of Lurch and the Bandana Kids. Keeping a low profile is keeping me alone. But who needs people? Einstein didn't. He had his theories for company, like I have mine.

The cold has emptied the streets, most kids having found a floor, the back seat of a car, or some nook or cranny to sleep in. As I walk, a window display of radio-controlled cars grabs my attention. Micha would go crazy if he got one of those for Christmas. I read a small sign attached to the inside of the door: Shoplifters Will Be Prosecuted. Yeah, well, that's only if they catch you. I smile grimly when I think of all the "gifts" I've ripped off over the years for Micha and Jordan. They deserve Christmas, too. Not just the rich kids.

Around the window are strings of small white lights that blink on and off. They remind me of that summer Granddad took me out late one night to see fireflies. I was so scared to go, but he coaxed me and folded my hand inside his huge one. Crickets chirped so loudly they nearly deafened me, owls hooted, and small animals scratched and rustled in the bushes. The air was wet and scented with pine. Then, over Grandma's garden, I saw tiny lights winking on and off.

It's their asses that light up. That's what Granddad said. Well, not in those exact words. He always said *bottom*. Granddad and Grandma didn't have asses, they had *bottoms* or *behinds*.

I read a book in the library all about fireflies and behinds. The female flashes her butt at the males and they flash back, trying to find a mate Not so different from humans, really, the girls wiggling their butts to attract the boys. In some firefly species, if the female doesn't like the male, she eats him. Again, not so different from humans.

I bet Einstein thought fireflies were mighty cool. I also think Einstein would say *ass*.

Snow begins to fall: large flakes, thick and soft and silent, covering the street, sidewalk, my shoulders, my eyelashes. It swirls about me as I move through it. Perhaps this is how Einstein saw particles of light, dancing, twirling about him, the air alive.

A car swishes past, black ribbons from its wheels parting the white blanket. A man lies prone on a park bench, a blanket and newspapers over him. Snow fills the valleys and gathers on the hills of his body.

At the old bank building, I gaze up at the gargoyles' stone heads. Capped with snow, they've lost their ferocity and look slightly ridiculous.

"Got somewhere to go for the night?"

A cop stands in front of me, bulky in his winter parka.

"Yeah." I look into his eyes.

"Where would that be?"

"A friend's place. Brad. He lives in a church. Or, it was a church. It's been converted into apartments," I add hastily.

"On your way, then."

I nod and stride away, trying to look like I have somewhere to go, where someone is expecting me. Except there is no place and there is no one. I jangle the change in my pocket, enough for one cup of coffee. I turn into a burger place, buy a coffee from a pimply-faced boy, and find a booth at the back. There's a clock on the wall over the counter and I sit facing it.

Eleven o'clock: Can I stretch the coffee out for an hour? It depends on how time moves in here—slowly, I'm guessing.

A couple of goth girls come in: black hair, black lipstick, whitened faces, dressed in long black coats and trailing black scarves. I've seen them on the streets before, chatted to them once or twice, but I don't make eye contact tonight.

Eleven-fifteen: I worry about Jordan. He's headed for trouble and I'm not there to straighten him out. Mom's no good at that kind of thing. How could she just throw me out? What did I do? I open a packet of sugar and dump it in my coffee, followed by a second and a third, hoping it'll give me a boost to keep me awake.

Eleven-twenty-five: I wonder if Grandma and Granddad are still alive.

Twelve o'clock: A drunk weaves his way among the tables, stinking of booze and vomit. Asks Counter Boy for a drink. Counter Boy reels back from the stench and tells him they don't serve alcohol. The drunk throws straws, condiments, and napkins. The Counter Boy retreats and picks up the phone. I slip into the washroom.

I slide down the wall and listen to the struggle outside.

Drunk shouts, cops placate him. Then silence. My eyes close drowsily. Maybe I'll just spend the night here.

"Did you want another coffee?" Counter Boy stands in front of me.

I stare at him blearily.

"Do you want another coffee?" Translation: Have a coffee or get out. I struggle to my feet, hoist my pack on my back, and, with a final glance at the clock, leave.

Twelve-ten: It's a new day. Why didn't Granddad try to find me? I wander aimlessly, keeping an eye out for cops and Vulture's people. I step into a doorway out of the wind.

Twelve-forty-five: The church clock chimes the quarter hour. Through the veil of snow, a figure climbs out of a car. Amber. She joins me in my doorway.

"Hey, Dylan." She greets me like a long-lost friend. Her legs are bare, her shoes are soaked, and the bottom buttons of her coat no longer fasten over her belly.

"Hi," I say.

I don't really want to talk to her. She's too annoying. But she's also the only person I've seen out tonight, and I suddenly feel a desperate need to use my voice.

"It's fucking cold," she says, hopping from foot to foot.

"When's the baby due?" I ask.

She grimaces. "In four months. It's hard to get anyone interested in you when you look like this." She thrusts out her belly and half laughs.

"Isn't there somewhere you can go? A home? You know, until the baby is born?"

"Go?" Her eyes widen in astonishment. "Fuck, Dylan. I'm a working girl. I owe Brendan for clothes and food. He's none too happy about the baby." She gestures down to her bulge. "That's why I'm out here in this fucking weather trying to make it up to him."

"Is Jenna *working* for him, too?" I ask.

A car approaches. Amber leaps from the doorway and strikes a provocative pose, but the vehicle goes by. She rapidly steps back beside me and hops from foot to foot again.

"Jenna? Oh, Jewel. She's not on the game yet. She's his fucking pet. Just like I was once." She says this without any bitterness.

"Can't you warn her?" I plead. "Tell her what it's really like. What Brendan's really like."

"And have Brendan beat the fucking crap out of me when he finds out?" Amber says. "I have to think of my baby."

"Think of your baby?" I repeat. "You're out here turning tricks. Smoking. Using—"

"Hey, what the fuck do you know about it?" Amber yells at me.

"I know that's not good for a baby," I say.

"Yeah, well, you would. Mr. Fucking High-and-Mighty-I-never-use-drugs, I don't-smoke, I-don't-say-goodbye." She comes close and pokes a finger into my chest. "You wait. Your turn will come. You haven't been out here long enough. It'll get to you, and you'll find yourself doing anything you can to make it go away." She pushes her face into mine. "It *is* getting to you, isn't it."

"Fuck you," I say.

"Yeah." She takes a step backwards. "My baby is none of your fucking business."

"What are you going to do when the baby comes? Are you giving it up for adoption?" I ask. I can't seem to let it go.

"No." Amber's face softens. She's still mad, but she likes talking about the baby. "I'm going to keep this one. I already gave one up. A boy. Children's Services made me. But I'm not letting them get their fucking hands on this one. That's why I'm staying right here on the street until this one's born. Once I have the baby, I'll be able to get some government money, get a place of my own. It'll be someone for me to love and someone to love me."

I pull off my toque and slap it on her head, and leave.

One o'clock: I'm freezing my ass off, then remember there's a hot-air vent in front of the office tower. I follow two sets of footprints in the snow down the sidewalk. Granddad took me one January afternoon to the bush out back of the farm and showed me animal and bird prints in the snow. Tracking, he called it. Tracking rabbits, squirrels, birds, deer.

"I wonder what kind of prints these are," he said, pointing to boot marks in the snow.

"Mine," I cried.

One-ten: A lighted sign over the office tower door flashes the time, then the temperature. I stare back at my prints, coming from nowhere, going nowhere.

One-twenty: Lukewarm air blows up from the vent. I climb inside my sleeping bag and lie on top of the hard metal strips, pulling my knees to my chest for extra warmth. I stuff my backpack under my head for a pillow. An orange light shines directly above me. I'm too visible, but I can't take the dark tonight. Not on top of the cold. Don't sleep, I warn myself.

One-thirty: Shit! I nearly fell asleep. I dig my fingernails into the palms of my hands to keep myself awake. Is my father tall? Thin? With black hair like mine? Grandma and Granddad didn't have any pictures of him in the house and they never spoke about him. It was like he'd died, or never existed for them. My mother had a few things to say about

him: useless bum, loser. She'd scream at me that I was just
like him. But I didn't know if she meant I looked like him, or
that I was a useless bum.

Two o'clock: Last year, Mom told Micha there was no
Santa. His face was white with disappointment, so I decided
to make Christmas. I stood in a line to register us to get a
turkey and some presents for Micha and Jordan. When I got
to the head of the line, I was told only an adult could register.
I told them my mother had pneumonia, and I described her
fever and cough. We got the turkey. We got the gifts. I told
Micha they were from Santa.

Two-fifteen: The air vent keeps my butt fairly warm, but
the top part of me is cold. Why did I give Amber my toque?
I'm so stupid.

Three o'clock: Snow swirls about me as the wind picks up. I
should leave this city. Get away from Vulture. Trouble's
coming. I can feel it. If I asked her, would Jenna go away with
me?

Three-fifty: My hand scrabbles under my head to make
sure my pack is there. I couldn't leave Micha and Jordan.

Four o'clock: An elderly man shuffles up to the vent. He
looks me over with rheumy eyes, breathes noisily through
red, toothless gums, then goes and pees a yellow stream
against the side of the office tower. He stumbles back to the
vent, curls up, and promptly falls asleep. I resent him being
here on my vent. I debate leaving, but I'm too tired.

Four-eleven: I get up and stamp my feet. Red-hot pins and
needles shoot through them. Despite the noise I make on the
metal slats, the old man doesn't wake. I pull the sleeping bag
over my head and lie back down.

Four-thirty: Jenna's hair on the back of my hand, silver
threads. I conjure up her face, her lips, her eyes. I imagine

her being mine. Taking care of her. I'd get a job and we'd have an apartment. I'd come home from work and Jenna would be at the stove. Stirring a pot. She'd turn and smile at me. And Micha and Jordan could come and stay. Maybe even live with us.

Five o'clock: A snowplow goes by and wakes me. The snow has stopped falling. I'm—so—fucking—tired. My face is wet. I might have been crying. I strive to see grey streaks in the sky, a promise of morning, but there's only black. The shortest day—the longest night—is in two weeks. I fish the Einstein book out of my pack and read by the orange light.

In 1898, Albert fell in love with a Hungarian classmate, Mileva Maric. My sluggish brain adds and subtracts. Einstein was seventeen. Mileva and Albert had an affair for three years and Mileva became pregnant. Mileva went to Hungary to have the baby, while Albert returned to Switzerland. Women didn't get abortions back then. Even birth control would be a problem. Mileva had a baby girl who was put up for adoption. Einstein and Mileva never saw the baby again. They got married the following year. I slam the book shut. What is the matter with people? Even back then they were giving away their kids. I wouldn't do that. I'd never give my kid away.

A hand shakes my shoulder. I pry my eyes open and see grey light, then the head of a cop comes into view.

Chapter 12

"Get up," the cop orders.

Feet entangled in my sleeping bag, I start to rise and nearly fall flat on my face. I kick the bag away and stagger upright. The world spins crazily. I feel weird—like I'm watching myself, outside of myself. My legs tremble and I worry that they won't hold me up.

A second cop prods the bundle of rags stretched out on the vent, and the old man rears up abruptly, spitting obscenities. He gathers his tatters about himself with an odd semblance of dignity and shuffles away.

I grab my pack and sleeping bag and make to follow him, but my cop grabs my arm and stops me.

"How old are you?" he asks.

"Eighteen," I reply.

"Let's have some ID," he says.

ID? You have to be someone, live somewhere, to have ID.

A few people push past us into the office tower, shooting quick, curious looks at me.

"Which of my credit cards do you want to see?" I ask.

"Don't be a smartass," the cop says.

There are times when my mouth separates from my brain and just goes on by itself. This is one of those times.

"There's my platinum MasterCard, or my gold American Express. Visa, perhaps?"

Shut up, I tell my mouth, *you're going to get me court-ordered into a group home.*

"Can I help?" Glen comes up beside me.

"Do you know this kid?" the cop asks.

"We've chatted from time to time," Glen says. "His name's Dylan . . ."

"Wallace," I quickly supply.

"Yeah, Wallace," Glen says. "I've never seen Dylan cause any difficulty here. He's not rude or intrusive. How would it be if I take him out for some breakfast? Get him out of your hair."

Breakfast. My mouth fairly drools at the word. I didn't have anything to eat yesterday and my ribs are sticking to my backbone, as Granddad would say.

The cops exchange glances.

"Here's my business card." Glen holds out a rectangle of white. The cop takes the card, studies it, stares at Glen, then back at the card.

"Well, if you want the trouble of looking out for him," he says. He faces me. "Get out of here and quit littering up the street."

Glen's face turns crimson. Mad-as-hell crimson. He opens his mouth but snaps it shut as the cops walk away.

"Well, thanks," I say. I kneel down to roll up my sleeping bag with hands that shake as if I'm eighty years old. My bladder is just about ready to explode, I need to pee so bad.

"What about that breakfast?" Glen says.

I get to my feet. "Breakfast?" I echo. My brain is barely functioning.

He starts to walk away and I follow.

"Don't forget your backpack," he says over his shoulder. Shit! I nearly left my life behind. I've never done that before. I'm obviously losing it.

I keep a few paces behind, uncertain about Glen, about breakfast. A block away, he stops and pushes a door open, and I follow him into bacon-scented warmth. My teeth chatter as I slide into a chair across from him.

"What can I get you?" a waitress asks, pen poised over a pad of paper.

"The full breakfast for one," Glen says. "Add an extra egg, glass of milk—"

"Coffee," I interject. It's my breakfast, after all.

"Milk and coffee." He folds the menu. "I'll just have a coffee."

She nods and leaves. I wonder if I could chase after her. Help fry up the bacon, scramble the eggs, so I could get it faster.

"Do you know the youth centre?" Glen asks.

I nod, because if I talk, the words will come out all cartoon-like between my clattering teeth. I try to hold my jaw still but I can't.

"They have showers there you can use. You need a hot shower to warm yourself up."

Shower. Water. Pee. I jump up and dart into the washroom and pee fast. Or at least I try. Peeing has a timetable of its own. I zip up and wring my hands together under the water faucet, then dry them on my pants.

The waitress and I arrive at the table at the same time, she with plates of food. I nearly fall over her to get to it. I cram egg, toast, bacon, and fried potatoes into my mouth, swilling it all down with coffee.

"Drink the milk, too," Glen says. "You're still growing."

I gawk at him. No one's ever cared about my growing. But there's another piece of bacon waiting, so I turn back to my plate.

I feel better now. Solid. The shaking has stopped. Little packets of jam sit in a basket in the middle of the table. Tearing three open, I spoon strawberry, raspberry, and marmalade onto the toast and savour the sweetness.

"You look more human now," Glen comments. He leans forward, elbows on the table, face intense. "Dylan, you're going to die if you stay out here on the streets."

My back stiffens.

"I'm not just talking through my hat here," he says. "I've had experience with this. I've seen it happen before." He slumps back, eyes haunted. There are ghosts locked inside him.

"You *look* clean." There's a question in his voice, but I don't give him anything. "Well, if you are, you won't be for long. Drugs, alcohol—it's all waiting for you. Is there any way you can patch up your differences with your parents? Go home?"

How do I patch up being thrown away? Beneath the table, my fingers clench, open, and clench again into fists.

"Is there anyone you can go to? A family member?"

"My grandparents." The words are out before I can snatch them back.

Glen picks up his coffee cup. The waitress materializes and refills it and mine. Glen looks pointedly at my milk, and I pick it up and drain the glass.

"Where do they live?" he asks.

"I don't know. On a farm," I add. "They took care of me for a while when I was little. They must be old now. They could be dead." I'm saying this more to straighten it out in my head than to tell Glen.

"Maybe we could find out," he says.

We? I stand up and pull on my coat. "Thanks for the breakfast," I tell him. I owe him that, but nothing else. Certainly not *we*.

"By the way, you're not litter," he says softly.

A wretched mixture of sleet and snow greets me when I leave the restaurant. Head down against the wind, I make my way to the youth centre. It will be empty at this time of the morning, and the shower idea sounded pretty good.

Ainsley is setting out soup bowls and napkins when I arrive. The only other person there is a kid hunched in misery over a table, leave-me-alone written all over him.

"Do you think I could have a shower?" I ask Ainsley softly. I don't know why I'm whispering. No one's here to know I'm filthy and desperate.

"Sure," she says. She leads me down a hallway and points out a room with two shower stalls and a change area. "Do you need a towel? Soap?" she asks.

"Soap," I reply. I'll dry myself on the scrap of towel from my locker. I don't want to ask for anything else today.

She hands me a bar of soap, then pulls a folded paper out of her pocket. "If you see Twitch later today, could you give him this?" She opens it, and I see a date written inside. "It's an appointment with a doctor for that cough of his. Would you be sure to tell him the date and time? Or send him to talk to me."

"Yeah," I agree reluctantly. What am I, Twitch's keeper?

I make the water as hot as I can stand it and let it flow over me. After a long time, I turn it off and dry myself. For one moment, I'm content. I'm warm, full, and clean. I grimace as I pull on dirty underwear, and the moment is gone.

I smooth my hair with my fingers, notice that it touches my shoulders, and squeeze the last of my toothpaste onto my sorry excuse for a toothbrush. Obviously, another trip to a drugstore is in order.

When I come out of the shower area, my heart leaps to see Jenna at a table talking to Twitch. I pull up a chair, telling my mouth to be cool and not say anything stupid.

"How's it going?" So far, so good.

Jenna nods hello, and yawns hugely. She looks like crap, but Twitch looks worse. His skin is a sickly yellow, except for two fiery red circles high on his cheekbones.

"Hey," he says, and breaks into a spasm of coughing.

I hand him the paper from Ainsley. "This is for you, an appointment with a doctor, though I think you should just go straight to the morgue," I say.

Fever-bright eyes widen anxiously.

"Kidding," I say. "Just kidding."

He glances at the paper and pushes it into his pocket.

"You have to go. You're really sick," I say.

"Yeah, yeah," Twitch says. He stands. "I'm going to see if the soup's ready."

He walks toward the kitchen area, and it's only Jenna and me.

"So," I say.

"So," she repeats.

"Cold out."

She yawns again.

I'm obviously dazzling her with my witty conversation.

She rests her head on the table. Silver hair hangs lifeless

around her face. There's nothing Madonna-looking about her today. It won't be long before Vulture has her working the streets, especially with Amber pregnant.

"Not getting any sleep?" I ask.

She swivels her head to look at me. "I was up late last night. And then Brendan wanted me at the church for morning mass. It's not like there's anybody there. It's too cold." Her eyes glance behind me. "Oh, shit!" She jerks upright.

I turn to see Lurch outside the door.

"He's come to collect Brendan's money," she says. "He won't be happy when he sees how little there is." She pushes back her chair and wearily pulls on her coat.

"Jenna, you should go home. It's just going to get worse out here." It flits through my brain that I sound an awful lot like Glen.

She glares at me. "You don't know what the hell you're talking about. I can't go home. I won't go home. And if anyone makes me, I'll run away again." She places both hands on the table and looms over me. "You don't know what it's like at my house," she says fiercely. "You don't know what happens there. *You—don't—know—anything!*"

Chapter 13

The city bus jerks away from the curb with a grinding shift of gears that opens my eyes. They immediately threaten to close again, made heavy by the heat and the swaying motion of the bus. It's quiet, with few people riding so early on a Saturday morning. I'm heading back to our house to see Micha and Jordan—and to ask my mother some questions. I begged last night in front of a restaurant for the fare, until the owner told me to clear off. Moving around from place to place to panhandle is getting annoying. I should just go back to the office tower. I gnaw on my thumbnail until it bleeds.

The bus is filthy: windows coated with grime, vinyl seats leaking grey stuffing like wool brains, the floor wet and slushy. A guy seated across from me tries to carve his initials into the metal back of a seat.

We weave past store windows hung with silver, red, and green tinsel. Christmas is nine days away. Twitch says it's a good time for us street kids because people get all warm-feeling and feed us until we burst. The rest of the year, they just want us to disappear.

Christmas at our house isn't any great shakes, none of that

family-warmth-laughter-decorations-stuff you see on television. But there is Micha's exuberance and Jordan's poorly concealed excitement.

My eyelids droop and I'm back at the centre with Jenna's face in mine. *You don't know anything!* Ainsley came over after Jenna left. "Someone's been misusing that girl," she said.

"Brendan," I replied.

"No, before that. At home, I think." Ainsley shook her head. "She shows all the signs of an abuse victim. You can't help her, Dylan, not until she wants to be helped. In the meantime, though, you could get yourself hurt. By both Jenna and Brendan."

I loomed over her like Jenna had loomed over me and yelled the same words. "You don't know anything!"

I haven't seen Jenna for close to a week now, and it worries me.

The bus passes the park near our house and I watch a couple kids in snowsuits sled down a small hill. It's tough going because the sun is rapidly melting the snow. I try to see their faces, wondering if one is Micha. But what am I thinking? Mom send the kids out to play? And in a snowsuit? That would be way beyond her. Saturday morning is when cartoons blare, kids bounce on the sofa, and cereal whizzes around the room, while Mom rests up from her strenuous week of doing absolutely nothing.

I pull the bus cord, the doors open, and I get off. Soon I'm in front of our house. There are Christmas lights strung in the window! I look wildly up and down the street to make sure I have the right house. I do. This can mean only one thing—they've moved!

The door opens and Jordan reaches out to grab a newspaper from the mailbox.

"Hey, man," he says, when he sees me. "How's it hangin'?"

"Good. How's it hangin' with you," I answer weakly, relieved they're still here.

"Hey, Mom," he yells over his shoulder into the house. "Dylan's here."

Jordan is yanked inside and my mother comes out, closes the door behind her, and stands on the step, arms folded across her chest.

"What do you want?"

My loving mother.

"I came to see my family," I say. "Can't a person visit their family? Especially so close to Christmas," I add.

"I don't want you here," she says. She glances nervously over her shoulder at the shut door. Dan must be in there.

"I want some information," I say. "And I want to see Jordan and Micha."

"Micha's out." She jerks her head toward the school. "He's playing."

My mouth drops open. "Wow! Turning into a proper mother, are you?" It sounds mean, which is exactly how I want it to sound.

The curtain moves in the window, and Jordan squashes his face against the glass, mouth open, his nose spread flat. I snort with laughter, and my mother whips around and gestures for him to leave.

"I'm not going away," I say.

She's between a rock and a hard place. Afraid of what Jordan might be saying inside to Dan, yet trapped outside by me.

"You can come in, but only for a minute," she says. "Then I want you to clear out."

She reaches for the doorknob but doesn't twist it. "Don't

screw this up for me, Dylan," she pleads. "Dan's a good guy. This could be a new start for me."

Yeah, right. Another new start. I shrug, not wanting her to see how rattled I am—by her plea, by Dan in the house, by the Christmas lights.

Suddenly, I'm barrelled over by a snowsuited Micha. I grip him hard and bury my face in his snowsuit, so no one will see the tears that run down my cheeks. Finally, I get control of myself and push him off me.

"We got Christmas lights, Dylan," Micha says. "Dan got them."

Wonderful Dan.

I follow my mother into the house and my mouth drops open. There, in the living room, is a Christmas tree. A fucking Christmas tree. All those years I wanted to get a tree for Micha and Jordan and she said no.

I glare at her and it's her turn to shrug.

A man comes out of the kitchen, apron tied over a substantial potbelly, grey hair sparse on his head, jowls sagging. He waves a spatula in my direction. "Who's this?"

"This is Dylan—" Micha begins.

"The boys' cousin," my mother says hurriedly.

Micha's eyebrows meet in the middle of his forehead, he's so shocked.

I wonder what my face looks like. My mother has just disowned me.

"Yeah, this is cousin Dylan." Jordan grins. He always was fast to recover.

Dan looks from face to face. He knows something's going on, but he's not sure what.

"Would you like some pancakes?" he asks heartily. Jovial type.

"He can't stay," my mother begins.

"Sure I can," I interrupt.

I lower my pack to the ground and throw my coat on the sofa. An empty sofa! Where's the usual pile of coats and laundry? Micha pulls off his new snowsuit and hangs it on a hook screwed into the wall by the front door. That's new, too.

"So you're Dan the man," I say. The guy who buys Christmas lights and tidies coats and couches—the guy who replaces me.

"Guess so." He disappears into the kitchen.

My mother grabs my arm. "You said you wanted some information. What?"

"I want to know where my grandparents live."

"I don't know," she says.

"Yes, you do," I reply. "They wouldn't leave that farm. We're the ones that did all the moving."

"If I tell you, will you go?"

"Maybe."

She bites her lip and leaves the room.

"Hey, why aren't you guys watching cartoons?" I ask. "It's Saturday. Where's the cereal?" The carpet is clean. "Who vacuumed this?"

"Mom did," Micha says. "Dan doesn't like dirt all over the floor. Look at this, Dylan. I made it at school." He points proudly to a red and green paper chain on the tree.

"It's cool, Micha." I touch it and a link breaks in my hand. "Sorry. Maybe we can glue it back together."

"That's okay, Dan'll fix it," Micha says.

I want to rip apart the whole fucking chain.

My mother comes back holding a letter. "Your grandmother died a while back," she says.

I'm stunned. "How long ago?"

"I'm not sure. Five—six years?" She hands me the letter. "It's just from the old man. There's a return address in the corner."

Turning it over, I see a rural address and a town, Murdock. The postmark is three years old. The letter has never been opened. Then I see the name on the letter.

"This letter was for me," I say.

"I didn't see any point in giving it to you."

"Just like you didn't see any point in telling me my grandma had died?" I want to hit her, I'm so mad. I take a step back so I won't.

"It wasn't like you were close to them," she says. "You hadn't seen them in years."

"And whose fault was that?" I yell.

Dan sticks his head around the door. "Pancakes are ready."

Micha runs into the kitchen. Jordan plops down on the sofa, face avid, longing for trouble.

"You said you'd go if I gave you the letter," my mother reminds me.

I stare at her a long moment. Her hair is clean, cut neatly. She's wearing jeans and a blouse instead of the usual food-stained sweatsuit.

"You said you'd go," she repeats. She licks her lips nervously.

"Those pancakes sound good." I shove the letter into my pocket. All deals are off! My mind is bouncing inside my head.

I sweep into the kitchen.

"Let me get some plates out for you, Dan." Crossing to the cupboard, I pull out dishes and glasses. I open the cutlery drawer and throw handfuls of forks and knives onto the table. "I know this place so well, Dan, you'd almost think I live here."

I open the refrigerator and grab the syrup, noticing the shelves crammed with food. This has to be Dan's doing. Mom never shops.

We sit down at the table, one big happy family. Dan places a large platter of pancakes in the centre and—holy shit—there are even sausages. I spear one with my fork and take a huge bite.

"You're quite the cook, Dan," I say. "Or maybe I should say, Uncle Dan. I hear you and Mo—, I mean, Aunt Joan here are getting hitched soon."

Dan puts a sausage onto Micha's plate. It shuts me up momentarily to see him feed Micha first, but I quickly regain my tongue. "That's quite a responsibility, taking on a whole family. Well, most of the family."

Dan slides a look at my mother, but she's flipping her fork over and over and doesn't meet his eyes.

"Yep, your aunt and I are getting married in the new year. How exactly are you related to Joan?" he asks.

"He's my sister's boy," my mother says quickly.

"That would be her sister Edith," I add. "She's the eldest. Aunt Joan here is the baby. Lots of family back in Murdock." I pick the name from the envelope. "Aunt Joan has four sisters and three brothers. But then, you'll meet them all at the wedding." I'm enjoying this. Making up an entire family.

"You've never told me anything about your family," Dan says to my mother. "I had no idea it was so large."

I watch gleefully, wondering how she'll get out of this one.

"We're planning a small wedding," my mother says, "with only immediate family coming, so Edith and the others won't be getting an invitation." *Nor will you,* her scowl says to me. She turns back to Dan. "I didn't see much point in telling you about them if they're not coming." Her fingers pleat the placemat—hell—placemats! I can tell she's dying for a cigarette. I bet she smokes on the sly.

I drown a pancake in syrup and stuff it in my mouth. It's good. Fluffy. "These are great, Uncle Dan. Good thing you can cook. Aunt Joan here can't boil water."

"Jordan, could you please get some milk," Dan orders quietly.

I've never met anyone so unflappable. But what's more shocking is Jordan opening the fridge to get milk. If I'd asked, he'd have told me where to go.

Dan cuts Micha's pancake into bite-sized pieces. It nearly tears me apart to watch.

"So, Micha. Do you know why the sky is blue?" I ask.

Micha shakes his head, mouth full of pancake and sausage.

"Well, light comes in waves, and when the sun shines on the earth, shorter wavelengths are scattered by the atmosphere. Blue light scatters more than other colours, so the sky looks blue."

Jordan snorts. "What are you now, a brainiac?"

I kick him, hard, under the table, just to remind him I'm bigger. "Einstein had a mathematical formula to explain why the sky is blue." I don't know why I'm going on about colours. I feel like I'm in a race, but I don't know how far or where the finish line is.

"That's interesting, Dylan. What grade are you in?" Dan asks.

"Well, Dan, I'm not at school right now. Aunt Joan can tell you all about that."

"Dan got us the Christmas tree," Micha says suddenly.

I put my fork down, appetite gone. I want to tell Dan who I am. I want my mother to tell Dan who I am. I want him out of my house and me back. But there's food on Micha's plate, more in the fridge, a new snowsuit, Jordan following orders, coats hung on hooks. Micha watches me anxiously. He wants to like Dan, but he's waiting to see if I like Dan before he'll allow himself to.

"It's a great tree, Micha. Awesome," I say. "You got a great tree, Dan." My voice cracks. I jump to my feet. "I just remembered, I have to be somewhere."

I rush into the living room, pull on my coat, and grab my backpack.

"You coming back for Christmas, Dylan?" Micha asks. He stands in the kitchen doorway, Dan's hands on his shoulders.

"You're welcome to come," Dan adds.

"I don't think so. I got that big family in Murdock waiting for me. You know how it is. Families." I'm babbling. How the hell do I know what it's like with families? I don't have one any more. My mother saw to that.

I open the door, but instead of going out, I cross the room in three long strides and pick up Micha and hug him.

"Bye, kid. You be good so Santa comes."

I set him down, wrap an arm around Jordan's neck, and crush his hair beneath my knuckles. I let him go, then barge out of the house, leaving the door open behind me.

Chapter 14

I walk and walk, seeing nothing around me, not knowing where I am or how much time has passed. And I don't care. Eventually, my legs refuse to go any farther. I sit on a bench at a bus stop, bury my head in my arms, and cry, huge sobs that shake my body. People and buses come and go, and still I sit, until I'm empty of tears. Then I remember my grandfather's letter.

Dear Dylan, I read. *I am not sure if this letter will find its way to you. You will be twelve years old now, nearly thirteen, and we have not seen each other for six years. I imagine you are a good size, as you always had large hands and feet to grow into.* I study my hands, bend and look at my feet. They seem normal. I picture myself, a small kid with monster appendages. *Your Grandma passed away a year ago and I miss her very much. It would give me a great deal of pleasure to see you again. I think of you often, and hope you are well, but as your mother has moved a few times, it's been difficult to keep track of you. I'm still here at the farm. I would like you to come and visit, and perhaps, if you want or need to, make your home with me. With love, your Grandfather.*

I can see him, sitting at the kitchen table, a pen held awkwardly in his shovel-sized hand, Grandma's chair across from him, empty. I can't believe my mother didn't give me this letter. I could have lived on the farm all this time. No dads, no uncles to hassle me. But would I have left Micha and Jordan? Who would have taken care of them? Maybe that's why Mom never gave me the letter. She needed me to be around. But if she needed me, why did she throw me out?

The sun paints the undersides of the clouds with a pink that fades as grey twilight gathers and softens the city's concrete edges. I don't want to be in this unfamiliar place in the dark. I climb on the next bus that comes and miraculously it heads toward downtown. Night falls rapidly now. The buses coming toward us are packed with people returning to warm homes. Gnawing at my thumbnail, I wonder where to go tonight. I could be at my granddad's.

I've barely stepped off the bus when Twitch materializes in front of me.

"Hey, Dylan, I found us a squat," he cries excitedly. Fingers, arms, legs, eyes move frenetically. Excited *and* high.

"Where?" I ask warily. Remembering Brad.

"It's an old factory," Twitch replies. "It has toilets."

"Are any surprises waiting there for me? Like Lurch?"

He hangs his head. "Sorry about that, man. No surprises. I promise." He solemnly crosses his heart, like Micha. Shit, he's so pathetic.

I follow him through dark streets and alleys to the edge of downtown. Here, it's empty stretches of asphalt, rusting car skeletons, broken streetlights, and long rows of warehousing. Figures hug the shadows, filling me with unease. An opening has been cut in a wire fence beneath a NO TRESPASSING sign. We crawl through and a factory rises before us, four storeys high with pale lettering barely visible against the dark brown brick: STOVEWORKS. A few windows on the first floor are boarded up, but the rest are jagged glass. We pass through a steel door hanging drunkenly from its hinges. It took a lot of strength, desperation, or anger to tear that door down. What is Twitch getting me into?

The first thing I notice is the stench. Damp, oil, burning wood, cigarette smoke, urine, and other odours I try not to think about. Twitch leads me up a set of iron stairs with no railing. It's as if they're suspended in space. I hug the wall, leery of the yawning black hole beside me.

The stink upstairs is worse. The first person my eyes fall on is the Swear Lady, with her shopping cart. How she got it up those stairs is beyond me. A small fire burns in the middle of the room. Dumb idea. This place is so old, it would go up in flames in a heartbeat. Twitch strides across the floor to where five people sit around the fire. Amber is one of them.

"Dylan," she cries.

Right about now, I really want to leave. But where would I go?

Torn blankets and stained pillows are laid out around the fire. A three-legged chair rests against a broken table. Someone has even pitched a tent. I hear rustles in the dark beyond the fire's light, sense movement, and realize there are more people. It's an eerie feeling.

As I walk slowly toward the fire, Amber suddenly screeches, "Watch the fucking hole!"

I look down to see broken floor planks framing a black space. Shit!

"You have to watch where you're going in here," Amber says as I come up to the fire. "There's a couple more." She waves a hand around vaguely, and I'm left none the wiser.

The floor is littered with empty food cans, beer bottles, hamburger wrappers, cockroach carcasses, and used needles. Those are a huge concern. A needle can pierce even the strongest shoe sole.

Twitch hunkers down beside Amber. "What do you think?" he asks me. "Not bad, eh?"

He breaks off to cough and spits into the fire. It hisses.

"Did you go to your doctor's appointment?" I ask him. I'm still standing, not sure if I'm staying or leaving.

"What?"

"The note I gave you. You had an appointment with the doctor today," I say. "Didn't you read it?"

"Oh. Yeah. I forgot to go," he says.

Amber reaches into Twitch's pocket and helps herself to one of his cigarettes. Most people would break her arm for that. She's lucky that Twitch is fairly agreeable. Amber lights up the cigarette and takes a deep pull.

"I thought you were cutting down," I say nastily.

"It's only my third one today," she replies, unruffled. "You fucking counting them?"

"I'm surprised to see you here. I thought you had a *room*." She brings out the best in me.

Amber takes a second drag from her cigarette and blows out a stream of white smoke. "I had to give up my room. I couldn't pay the rent. Brendan cut me loose. I'm too pregnant to turn tricks."

No use to him any more. But Jenna is.

I feel sick.

"Where are the toilets?" I ask.

Twitch gestures into the blackness past the hole in the floor. "Over there."

I'm afraid to move into the dark.

"Here." He tosses me a flashlight. "I picked this up at the hardware store." Meaning, I walked in, picked it up, and left—without paying.

I press the button on the side and a pool of weak yellow

light shines on the floor in front of me. Then I just follow my nose. I'm gagging before I even reach the bathroom. I play the light over the room. Then wish I hadn't. There are toilets, like Twitch promised, but he forgot to mention they didn't flush. I don't want to go in there, but my kidneys are about to burst. I take a huge breath, run in, turn off the flashlight, quickly do my business, and run out, retching.

I unroll my sleeping bag and lay it next to the fire. I won't sleep, I tell myself, just rest until morning, then I'll leave. I'm scared of the people lurking in the shadows, scared of the fire, scared of the dark, just—scared!

My eyes close. Don't sleep! I force them open to see Twitch with a needle up his arm. They close again, but raised voices and the sound of flesh meeting flesh jerk me awake. It's over quickly. No one has spare energy to fight. In the dark, small pinpricks of light—eyes, rats' eyes—stare back into mine.

Amber pushes a guy off her. "Asshole," she mutters.

The moans, grunts, murmurs, and yellow firelight shape my dreams, and I'm restless all night.

Next time my eyes open, watery light filters through broken windowpanes to show a man peeing in the corner. So much for the toilets! The fire's dead and Twitch lies next to it, unconscious and shivering. The humane thing to do would be to cover him with my sleeping bag, but I roll it up and tie it to my pack.

Picking my way over bodies and garbage, I skirt the holes in the floor and hug the wall as I go down the stairs. Through the broken door and the hole in the fence. The stink of the place clings to my clothes and I recognize it now. Desolation.

Chapter 15

I sit in Mandy's with a cup of coffee, and the wedding photograph of Grandma and Granddad on the table in front of me. I'm hoping one or both of them will make me feel normal again after my night in the factory. It settles me to see the grey blossoms, the woman fanning herself, and Grandma and Granddad in their wedding clothes. I touch the figure of Grandma with a trembling finger. Her face is fuzzy in my mind, but I remember clearly the clicking of her knitting needles, and her voice telling me not to go near the well and to eat my beans.

I drain my cup and use the washroom in the restaurant—I am a patron, after all—to rinse my face before I leave. The wedding photograph has planted an idea in my brain, and by the time I arrive at the library, it has taken shape. I pull on the large glass doors, but they don't budge. I try again, disbelieving. The library is always open. Except on . . . Shit! It's Sunday. My idea is all shot to hell. Or is it?

Searching through my pack, I find the flyer about the school for street kids. *The school's computer lab can be used for e-mail, school or job searches,* I read, and, most important, it is open on Sundays. As I'm reading the flyer, a new theory comes to me. About Twitch. But I will need to prove it.

The school is in an old store, like the youth centre, but it has bars on the windows and a surveillance camera over the door. I smile widely for the camera and step inside. Ten computers are set along one wall. Tables and chairs stretch down the middle of the room. The opposite wall has floor-to-ceiling shelves full of books and magazines. The first person I see is Mr. Crowe, bouncing on the balls of his feet. It's surreal seeing him here.

"Why, Dylan. I thought you'd moved," he says.

"Change of plans," I reply.

"You're looking dreadful."

There's no disputing that. "What are you doing here?" I ask.

"I help out with the school on weekends."

From a room in the back, Glen walks out. I want to leave, but my feet won't go. My idea has made them take root.

"Hello, Dylan. I haven't seen you for a while," Glen says.

"What exactly is this place for?" I ask.

"It's an alternative for kids who need a different kind of schooling," Glen tells me. "Regular schools aren't for everyone. Lots of kids slip through the cracks. Here we offer those kids literacy skills, a chance to get a high school diploma, correspondence courses, and access to computers to do job searches, do up resumés. We're trying to give street kids tools to build their lives."

He sounds like an advertisement.

"Can I use a computer to do—research?" I ask.

"Sure. All we ask is that you fill out this form first." He slaps a piece of paper down on a table and pulls out a chair for me. I sit and read it over. Name—first only, if you prefer. Reason for using computer. Time you log on, time you log off.

"It's to keep track of how much the computers are used," Glen explains. "It helps to have concrete figures when you're asking for corporate support." He wanders off and begins to sort books on a shelf.

I pick up a pen, fill out the form, and hand it to Mr. Crowe.

"We'll get you on this one," he says, pointing to a computer.

"I thought this was a peer tutor set-up," I say. All these adults hovering around are making me nervous.

"It is," Mr. Crowe replies. "Glen and I are volunteer support staff. At the moment, none of our tutors are in. Glen's company donated most of these computers and puts up the rent money."

I can't help wondering—why?

"Well, I know you can find your own way from here," Mr. Crowe says, and he leaves me alone.

I use a search engine and enter the town name: Murdock.

And there it is, on a map right in front of me. Murdock. And suddenly I can see the farm, Granddad crossing the yard to the barn, stopping to sniff the weather, calling back to Grandma. A small face is in a window, watching him. Me. I smell lemon furniture polish, fried onions, baking bread, dry grass, ripe pears, honeysuckle, and hollyhock. I've travelled back in time. Part of my brain wonders idly what Einstein thought about time travel. Did he believe in it? I do.

Reluctantly, I wrench myself back to the present.

I check further. Population: 1000. Primarily an agricultural area. Five and a half hours northeast of here. Bus service, no train. I go to the telephone directory website and type in my granddad's surname, Wallace. It takes me a minute to remember his first name. Edward. Then the town. And there is his phone number. I think I'm going to puke!

"How's it going?" Glen asks. He puts a hand on my shoulder.

I stiffen, and he casually removes it.

"Good," I say. And suddenly, I want to share this with him, with anyone. "This is my grandfather's telephone number." I go back a website. "And here's where he lives."

Glen bends and looks at the screen. "Murdock. I've been through there before. It's a pretty place." He straightens. "So what do you want to do?"

At first, I think he means with the computer, then I realize he means with the information. "I don't know," I say.

"Do you want to call him?"

"No."

"Go see him?"

Yes, I desperately want to see the farm. See my grandfather. Be safe. But I'm scared. It's been nearly ten years.

Glen pulls out a chair next to mine and sits. "You'd need to take the bus," he says. "I'll help you with the fare—" I start to protest, but he waves it off. "It's not a gift. You'll have to work it off. Think of it as an advance on your pay."

"Pay? What kind of work?" I ask.

"We could use you in here. We need more peer tutors. Alex"—he nods toward Mr. Crowe—"says you're good with computers. You'll have to take the three-day training course that all our volunteers take before you start. And then you can help out in my office. That's the paying job. You'll run errands and sort mail. We'll work out the details on paper— how much you keep for yourself, how much you pay back on your debt. And you'll have to sign it, like a contract."

"You can hire me?" I say. "Don't you have to check with someone—like your boss?"

"It'll be fine," he assures me.

I study the computer screen a long time. It's a commit-ment, and I don't like commitments. But it is a way to see my grandfather.

"Why would you do that?" I ask. "Buy a bus ticket for me. Give me a job."

"Because I think you're intelligent, worthwhile, and full of potential. I want to get you off the streets"—his face tightens—"before something happens to you. What do you say?"

I gnaw at my raw thumb, brain spinning. "I need to think about it."

Chapter 16

A week later, Glen and I are at the bus station to buy the ticket. That was the limit of my endurance of the factory.

The station reeks of disinfectant, but it can't disguise the odour of years of unwashed bodies and greasy french fries. We join a long line at the ticket counter, and I look around while we wait. The Garbage Man is rooting inside a bin. I'm surprised they let him do that here, but he's causing no harm. A group of kids, the oldest maybe thirteen, taunt him, but he's oblivious. Or appears to be. What is beneath the garbage bags, the multiple layers of clothes, the skin of the Garbage Man? What does he think? Feel? Could he actually be a genius like Einstein? More likely his thoughts plod in the same groove day by day, ruled by his obsession with garbage.

"Huh?" We're at the front of the line and Glen is speaking to me.

"I said, I can get you a ticket for this evening, but you know it's Christmas Eve," he repeats.

"Oh, gee, I had plans for a real down-home family Christmas," I say. "But that's okay, I can change them."

Glen rolls his eyes and turns back to the counter.

A few minutes later, I have a printed ticket in my hand.

As we leave the bus station, Glen hands me a business

card. "This is mine. You can reach me here." He pulls it back. "Just a minute." He writes on the back of it. "And this is my home phone. Keep in touch, and let me know how it goes in Murdock. Feel free to call collect," he adds.

I put the card into my pocket.

"Are you sure you don't want to call your grandfather and let him know you're coming?" Glen asks. "That's a long way to go to find he's not there."

"I'm sure. He wouldn't leave the farm. It'll be a surprise. A Christmas gift." That's what I say, but really I'm afraid Granddad will tell me not to come.

Glen slaps my shoulder. "Well, I'm off. I hope it works out for you. But don't forget, that ticket isn't a gift. You have to work it off starting in the new year."

"Glen," I croak. I have something else to ask, but it's hard. "Yeah?"

"Can I work off more than this?" I ask, waving the ticket.

"What do you mean?"

"I guess I mean, can I have another advance? Just a small one." I look at the sky, the pavement, the buildings, anywhere but at Glen. "I want to get something for my brothers. For Christmas, you know." I haven't even thanked him for the ticket, and already I'm asking for more!

"What sort of gifts did you have in mind?"

"Well, I saw this remote-control car for Micha. He'd think that was pretty cool," I say quickly. "And Jordan. He'd like a portable CD player, but they're kind of expensive."

"Where did you see this car?"

"Two blocks down. At the electronics place."

"Well, we can go look, but I'm not promising anything," Glen cautions.

At the electronics store, people are jammed shoulder to shoulder checking out the goods. Christmas music blasts out of speakers. A man pays for a television set and CD player, and I'm jealous as hell of the person who is getting those gifts. I plow through the people to the front window, Glen in my wake, and point out the red car.

"How old's Micha?" Glen asks.

"Six."

"You're right. He would like that," Glen says. "Fine. You go ahead and get one for him."

As I pick up the car, I imagine the joy on my little brother's face.

"And Jordan?" Glen asks.

"He's ten."

We bend and look at a glass counter full of CD players.

"There's no point in getting the cheapest one," Glen says. "It'll be broken before Christmas Day is over. How about that one?" He points to a silver case.

Suddenly, I think this is a bad idea. I'll be working the rest of my life for Glen. But Micha's excited face is right there in front of me, and Jordan's eyes when he sees the CD player, and I wonder what Dan got them.

Glen indicates our choice to the sales clerk and pulls out a credit card. I push through the crowds and look at the new CD releases rather than watch the sale go through. I've got a couple of my favourites in the bottom of my pack but nothing to play them on.

Glen comes up, pocketing the bill. "We'll add that to your total amount owing," he says.

"I will pay you back, man," I tell him. "I'm not shi— I'm not kidding you."

"I know," Glen says. "I wouldn't do this otherwise."

Now I really do have to pay him back, because he's acting like he believes in me. This is why I don't like being obligated.

We push out of the store to the sidewalk.

"Now, I need to go buy my wife something," Glen says.

"Thanks for this." I hold up the bag.

"Hey, if we hadn't bought them, you'd have just stolen them." He grins. "This way, I keep you honest." He holds out a second bag. "This is for you, from me. This one you don't have to pay back."

I take the bag, open it, and see a second CD player.

"I hope you have some music to listen to," he says. "It's a very long trip to Murdock."

Shit! I'm going to cry. In the middle of the street with people all around, I want to lay my head down on this man's shoulder and bawl my eyes out like I'm a baby. And worse, I think Glen knows.

"I hope everything goes well for you. Merry Christmas," he says briskly, and he's gone before I can thank him.

I stuff the gifts into my pack—like Santa, I tell myself—and I feel good. I have a bus ticket, somewhere to go for Christmas, presents, and, most important, I have a plan—to take Jenna with me to Murdock.

As I walk, I work out the details. I'll exchange Glen's ticket for two others to take Jenna and me as far as we can get, then we'll hitchhike the rest of the way to Murdock. I'm not sure what Glen would think of my plan, but as the end result is the same, he doesn't need to know. I can see Jenna in Granddad's kitchen, filling Grandma's empty chair, hair shining silver, and his surprise and delight that we're there. But first I have to find her.

The youth centre is crowded. Twitch sits at a table with Amber.

"Hi," I say as I ease my pack from my shoulders, pleased with the weight of it, the presents inside.

"Hi yourself," Amber replies.

Twitch says nothing, and I notice how unnaturally still his legs and arms are. So still, I know he's sick. Really sick.

A blast of cold, damp air whips both our heads around to see the Bandana Kids come in.

"Hey." The leader of the posse comes over and punches my shoulder. Hard. "Long time no see. How are you doing? Making any money?" They burst into laughter.

"Leave him alone, you fucking assholes," Amber says.

"Shut up," I tell her.

I begin to get to my feet, but a hand on my shoulder pushes me back into my chair.

"Hi, Dylan," Ainsley says. She turns to the Bandana Kids. "You're just looking for trouble, so get lost, boys." She jerks her head toward the door.

They flip me the finger but leave, as she asks.

"Something special for Christmas Eve." Ainsley sets a steaming cup of apple cider and a plate of cookies in front of me, then glances worriedly at Twitch. "You sure you don't want anything?" she asks him.

He shakes his head.

I remember then my theory about Twitch. Bus tickets and presents temporarily pushed it out of my head.

"He didn't go to his doctor's appointment," I tell her.

"So I gather," Ainsley replies. "Did you tell him the date and time?"

"I gave him the note," I start to say.

"I'm fine," Twitch breaks in. "I just need a . . ."

His voice trails off, but I know what he was going to say.

He needs a fix. Medicine up his nose, down his throat, or in his veins that makes him better. For a little while, anyway.

"You need a doctor," Ainsley says flatly. "And you,"—she turns to Amber—"need to quit smoking."

Amber pulls a face as Ainsley walks away.

"Look at this, Twitch," I say grandly. I pull out the bus ticket, put it down on the table, and tap it. "Read that." Time to prove my theory.

Twitch glances at it and nods.

"No, I mean read it."

Twitch pulls it closer to him and lowers his head. I see his lips move. He shoves it back.

"You don't even know what it is, do you?" I say.

Twitch looks over my shoulder out the door. "I know what it is. A ticket."

Amber reaches for the ticket, but I pull it away from her and push it back across the table to Twitch. "To where? Read it. Out loud."

"I don't have to read it," Twitch says. "I don't give a shit."

"You're the lousiest liar," I say. "You don't know what it's for because you can't read." I say this triumphantly, though a part of me wonders why I need to have this particular theory proved.

Anger flickers in his eyes. "So what? You came in here just to piss me off? Well, you did, so go away," he says.

I grab a couple cookies and scramble to my feet, picking up my pack.

I walk to the back of the room, where Ainsley sits at a desk, a textbook open in front of her.

Amber trails behind me. "That was a shitty thing to do," she says.

"Get lost." I don't need her telling me. I know. But I was so wrapped up in proving my theory, I didn't think any further. "And I don't need you butting into my life," I add. "I can take care of myself."

Now it's Amber flipping me the finger as she heads toward the washroom.

"Have you seen Jenna?" I ask Ainsley.

She lowers the textbook. "Amber's right. That was a mean thing to do to Twitch. Everyone knows he can't read. That's why I told you to tell him the appointment date and time."

"I didn't know that—then," I say. I'm getting pissed off now. "Have you seen Jenna?"

Before she can speak, the door opens again. A female police officer comes in, glances around the centre, and walks back to us. I move to one side, but close enough to overhear. I'm surprised to see how blank Ainsley's face has become. Then I remember. Ainsley was a street kid once.

The policewoman holds out a picture to Ainsley. "Have you seen this girl?"

Ainsley studies the photograph, then hands it back without a word.

It's pointed in my direction, and I see Jenna smiling at me. "You seen her?"

I shake my head.

She turns back to Ainsley. "So, she's not been in here?"

"Not recently," Ainsley says carefully.

"And if you had seen her, you wouldn't tell me anyway."

"You drag her back home, you know she'll just run again."

The policewoman pockets the photograph without comment.

"Are there other children in the family?" Ainsley asks.

"I don't know."

"Are the parents being investigated?"

"I don't know that, either," the officer says. "Why?"

"Something pushed that girl out the door."

The officer regards Ainsley a long moment, nods, and leaves. Ainsley goes back to her textbook.

"What are you doing?" I ask.

"Studying," she says shortly.

"For what?"

"I'm taking courses to be a social worker," she says, voice defiant.

"To be one of them?" I'm incredulous. I thought Ainsley was one of us.

"Look at him." Ainsley stabs a finger at Twitch. "And then there's Amber. The way I see it, their problems should be straightened out long before they get to this point. To being on the street, to being high all the time, abused. If we could get to the problems earlier, help families sooner, we might stop this."

"How?" I ask.

"I haven't figured that out yet," Ainsley admits. "But I think these"—she points to the books—"might be the first step. They try, Dylan. It's just such a huge job."

Amber wanders back over. "You'll find Jenna at Holy Rosary," she says. "It's Christmas Eve and noon hour Mass will be packed. Brendan won't want to pass that up." She laughs loudly. "You're such a fucking lovesick puppy."

I push past her and leave without saying goodbye to any of them. Outside, I cram the cookies into my mouth. They're shortbread. I hate shortbread.

Like Amber said, Jenna is in front of the church. Her lips are blue and her entire body shakes with cold. She's thin, tired, dirty. She now looks like she lives on the street.

As I gaze at the church behind her, stained-glass windows and soaring spires, I get one of those rare instances of enlightenment when colours dazzle, edges become razor sharp, time freezes, and you know something important is attempting to shove itself into your brain. Einstein experienced these moments. I know that for a certainty, because I can see it in his face.

What's shoved itself into my head is that it's unfair. Grossly unfair. The huge cathedral of goodwill, riches, Christmas joy and peace, and Jenna at the gate, begging. In that eerie otherworld of enlightenment, I travel through past ages and see ragged, hungry people sitting at the gates of cathedrals all over the world. It's been like this forever. It will always be like this. My shoulders droop beneath the weight of my thoughts.

"Why are you staring at me?" Jenna asks.

The world returns to normal.

"Just thought I'd tell you, I'm going away for a few days," I say casually. I need to do this right. Not scare her off.

"You are?"

"Yeah. I'm going to see my grandfather. He lives in Murdock. It's about five hours north of here."

She glances at the clock between the spires. "This must be the longest church service ever. When are they coming out? I'm freezing my ass off."

I wonder if she's heard me.

"How are you getting there?" She has.

"Bus. I have a ticket."

She wraps her arms around herself for warmth. "So you're going away for Christmas. I'll miss you."

It's the opening I need. "Look, why don't you just blow this off?"

"I can't." She looks nervously up and down the street. "Brendan wouldn't like that."

"Who cares what Vulture likes?"

"Stop calling him that," she says. "I owe him money for food, clothes."

I hunker down beside her. "Yeah, I know. That's what he does to people. He makes you owe him, and then you're his. He's a parasite. He lives off other people."

"But he's been good to me," Jenna argues weakly. "No one messes with me when they know I'm with Brendan."

"Is he good to you when he slaps you around? When he makes you work for him but doesn't give you enough money to live on? Look at Amber. She was just like you. He used her, and now she's no good to him, so he cuts her loose. She got pregnant working the streets for him."

She stares down at her shoes. I know she's smart, so why can't she see this? Is she that scared? I want to shake her.

She climbs to her feet. "Let's go." She opens her hand and flashes a twenty-dollar bill. "Brendan doesn't know about this. I earned it myself. You hungry?"

What a question.

"Whatever you want. My treat."

She tucks a cold hand inside mine and I'm in heaven.

We get fries, burgers, and drinks at Mandy's.

"How did you get the money?" I ask.

Jenna giggles. "This guy came up to me on the street and asked if he could see my boobs for ten bucks. I figure, why not? He's just looking. So we go into this alley and I lift my T-shirt and he says if I let him touch one, he'll give me twenty dollars." She takes a sip from her drink. "I guess you can say I got a boob job." She laughs.

I push my plate away, feeling ill. "You should be more

careful. Going into an alley with some guy. Shit! You could have been hurt."

She'll never do that again if I get my way. I lean over the table. "Come to Granddad's with me for Christmas," I say.

"What?"

"I'll take my ticket back and I'll get two. We'll go as far as we can, then we'll pick up rides the rest of the way. You'll like my granddad."

"I don't know." Jenna plays with her fries.

"Vulture will have you hustling on the street soon and all the money will go to him. You want to be working the streets?"

She won't meet my eyes, and my heart sinks. She's already been out there. What was it? A hand job? A blow job?

"It doesn't matter how much you work for him, you'll never pay him off. He won't let you. That's how pimps work. I'd never do that to you."

Now she does look at me. "I know you wouldn't. You're sweet, Dylan," she says.

And that makes me feel like a fraud. Am I doing this because I'm sweet? Or amazingly selfish?

"Okay. I'll go with you to Murdock." She smiles, and her face is radiant.

My heart flops over.

"What time do we leave?" she asks.

"Five o'clock this evening. Meet me at the bus station at four. I'll see to the tickets." I scramble to my feet. Elated. "I got to go. I have stuff to do this afternoon, but I'll see you later, right?"

"Four o'clock," she promises.

I bend and kiss her lightly on the lips.

Chapter 17

Cheese stretches in long strings from the pizza in my hand to my mouth. Hamburgers, fries, and pizza. This is the most food I've had in months, and all in one day. To get bus fare, I stood at the double doors of the mall, and right away some guy gave me ten dollars. Christmas generosity, I guess. The bus comes and I shove the remainder of the savoury mess into my mouth and climb on. I'm going to drop off Micha and Jordan's gifts. A black cloud threatens to lower over me as I realize I won't see them Christmas Day. *You'll be with Granddad,* I tell myself. *And Jenna.* And the cloud lifts.

At the house, I am uncertain whether or not to walk in, so I ring the bell. The curtain moves in the window, and then the door opens a crack. "Yes?" my mother says, like I'm a complete stranger.

"I brought some Christmas gifts for Micha and Jordan," I say.

The door opens wider. She glances quickly up and down the street. "Okay. Leave them with me. I'll see they get them."

"I want to give them to them myself," I say.

"They're out with Dan."

"I'll wait. Can I come in?"

"No," she says. "Leave the gifts with me."

I sit down on the step. "I'll stay here until they come."

"Why are you so much trouble?" she asks. "All your life you've been trouble. Dan had a lot of questions about you after you came last time. You and your big mouth."

"Did you tell him I was your firstborn?" I say.

"Jeezus," she says. She goes back in, leaving the door open, so I follow her.

"I need my sweaters." I head toward the bedroom I shared with Micha and Jordan.

"I put your stuff in boxes in the basement."

That stops me dead. She's erasing me from the family. I forget the sweaters and pull the remote car and CD player from my pack and place them under Dan's Christmas tree.

"You steal those?"

"No. I have a job," I tell her.

"What kind of job?"

"I'm a tutor at a computer lab," I say grandly. "Actually, I have two jobs. I also sort mail for a company downtown."

Her eyes narrow as she takes in the gifts. "Must pay well," she says.

I shrug as I wander through to the kitchen and help myself to a pop from the fridge. "So what did you tell Dan about me?"

She perches on the edge of a chair. "That you're my sister's boy."

"Nothing like starting out a marriage with complete honesty," I say.

"I'll tell him when the time's right."

I snort at that, and the carbonated fizz tickles my nose, making me sneeze.

"I wish you'd leave," she says.

"I want to see Micha with his car," I tell her. Stubbornness runs in the family. "I'm going to Murdock this evening."

She flinches, as if I've hit her. "Why?"

"I'm going to see my granddad."

"I hate that place and everything to do with it," she says. "You're better off staying away."

"What did he ever do to you?"

"What did he and his wife ever do *for* me?" she replies.

"What about your parents? You want me to look them up for you? If they live there any more, that is."

"Oh, they'll be there. They'd never move away. They don't like change."

"Didn't you ever want to see them? Show off us kids?" I ask, curious about these grandparents I've never met.

My mother jumps to her feet, reaches into the back of a cupboard, and takes out a cigarette package. She taps one out, lights it, then opens the kitchen door to let the smoke out.

"Something else you haven't told Dan about?"

She grimaces. "I'm trying to quit. But there are some things that drive me back to them. Like you. Or thinking about my parents." She releases a stream of white smoke into the cold. "Real Bible-thumpers, the pair of them. Wanted me to be quiet and nice, keep my blouses buttoned to my neck, my skirts over my knees."

She takes another drag. "Everything was a sin with them. Dancing, music, smoking, laughing. It was a sin to be alive. I put up with it at first, but then I went insane. Everything they thought was a sin, I did it. They'd lock my door and I'd climb out the window. They nailed it shut and I pulled the nails out. I found the wildest boy in town, your dad, and went out with him. Then you came along." She glares at me like I'd suddenly arrived on her doorstep one day just to ruin her life. "They wouldn't help me. Told me I'd made my bed, so go lie on it. That's real Christian charity for you. And your dad, he just cut out. Left me alone."

"But Grandma and Granddad. They helped you. I remember them buying me stuff, letting me stay with them."

"The kind of help I needed was money and they wouldn't give me any. Said I wasn't responsible enough. The money wouldn't benefit you. You stayed with them a bit, but I couldn't get any money from the government if you weren't with me, so I had to keep you. I told them if their son didn't pay support, they should pay if they wanted to see you, and they wouldn't. Guess they didn't want you that bad." She smirks, and I hate her more than I've ever hated her before.

"Tell Micha and Jordan I said Merry Christmas. Give them their gifts." I don't want to be in that house with her another minute.

"There's smoke in here," I yell back over my shoulder as I walk through the living room, though I can't really smell anything. But she'll air it out, and Dan will wonder why the house is so cold, and there will be more questions.

The city bus crawls downtown, people getting on or off at every stop on the route. My thumb is just about gnawed off by the time we arrive. I sprint the two blocks to the bus station, burst through the doors, and discover I'm ten minutes early. I debate exchanging my ticket but decide to wait until I find Jenna. The station is packed with holiday travellers, and I push my way through them, checking both entrances. No Jenna. By four-fifteen, the pizza in my stomach has begun to churn. I leave the station and look up and down the sidewalk, but there's no sign of her there, either. The lineup at the ticket gate stretches deep into the station, and I should exchange my ticket, but I complete another circuit of the waiting room instead. I'm like Twitch. I can't keep still.

Finally, a loudspeaker announces boarding for the bus to Murdock. I do another frenzied search around the waiting room, then go to the gate. I think I knew deep down that I would go alone.

Chapter 18

The rain turns to sleet and then snow the farther north we travel. I stare out the bus window at houses lit with strings of coloured lights, imagining the excited kids and decorated trees inside. When I was little, I thought Christmas was beer bottles and fights, until television told me otherwise. Christmas is supposed to be about basted turkey, grandparents, and presents—lots of presents. One year, I discovered a turkey in our fridge. I decided to cook it myself, because then the rest of Christmas would all fall into place. Mom and an uncle, I can't remember which one, were sleeping in the bedroom, so I cranked the temperature on the oven as high as it could go, dropped the turkey in a pan, and shoved it in. Hours later, Mom woke up screaming the house was on fire. Jordan and I were in the basement playing and hadn't noticed the smoke billowing from the kitchen. How the hell was I supposed to know the plastic wrapper had to come off the turkey? For Christmas that year I got a sore ass that I couldn't sit on for a week.

A small part of me hopes that Dan works out, for Micha and Jordan. But it's a really small part. Mostly, I want Micha and Jordan to need me. If they don't need me, well, I guess

I'm—nothing. No good to anyone. I poke my reflection in the eye. Even Jenna knows I'm nothing.

Why didn't she come to the bus station? Was it something as basic as my body odour? I sniff myself. I stink, but no worse than usual. It was the kiss! I shouldn't have kissed her. Stupid bad-breath kiss. Maybe that's why Einstein's girl-friend, Mileva, moved to Hungary without him. He gave her a bad-breath kiss and she thought, yuck! Except Mileva was having a baby, so at least Einstein got to have sex with her.

Outside now are long stretches of black, broken sporadi-cally by a lighted window. Dread knots my stomach. Will Granddad want me? Why did I leave the city for all this dark? I shift over on the seat away from the window and watch the headlights slice through the dark and snow. The driver catches my eye in the mirror. "A white Christmas," he says. "Though the driving will be hell if this keeps up."

I nod. His eyes flick to the road, then back again to me. "You the one going to Murdock?"

I nod again.

"Too bad. I could have gone right home to the family, but Murdock takes me half an hour out of my way."

"Sorry," I say.

I slide back toward the window and dig out the CD player Glen gave me, feel a moment's dismay when I realize it needs batteries, then find a pack of them in the bag, too. He thought of everything. I slip in a CD, press the plugs into my ears, and lean back, hoping the music will push all the thoughts out of my brain.

Doesn't happen.

Glen. I don't get him. Why does he bother with me? Why did he give those computers to the lab? What does he get out of it? I find his business card and turn on the light over my seat to read: Glen Matthews, President, TechSystems.

TechSystems! They're huge. They have the entire top four floors of the office tower! Maybe it's a fake. I run my fingers over the embossed name. The card's real. He's president! I put the card away, lean back, and try to concentrate on the music.

Real Bible-thumpers, Mom called her parents. I have an image of a man and woman whacking the hell out of their Bibles. *Thump! Thump!* Up the stairs to my mother's bedroom. *Thump! Thump!* Lock her in so she can't live. No wonder she's so nuts. I should look them up just to give them a glimpse of what they did to their daughter. Show them *me*!

I pat my coat pocket to reassure myself the return ticket is still there. That was a bit of a surprise, when the bus driver handed me back a portion of the ticket.

I must have dozed off, because next thing I hear is a man yelling, "Murdock."

Half asleep, I gather up my things and crawl down the bus steps into the snow and wind and cold. The doors shut behind me and the bus leaves in a cloud of fumes. I stare after it, feeling abandoned. It had become a safe cocoon.

I've been let off in front of a small store. The lights are on, so I go in. It's an everything store, selling groceries, cards, cosmetics; doubles as a post office and, it seems, is also the bus station.

"You it?" a man's voice asks.

"Huh?" I don't see anyone.

A shiny pink head with a fringe of white hair pops up from behind a counter. "You the only one off the bus tonight?"

"Yeah," I say.

"Good. I can close up then."

But where do I go?

"Do you know Edward Wallace's place?" I ask the man.

"Yep. You go north out of town about ten minutes, turn left on the Old Cowpath Sideroad. Second farm on the right." He studies me over the top of his glasses. "That's ten minutes by car. Longer if you're walking."

I stare out the store window at the drifting snow. I was so busy getting here, I never thought about what I'd do when I arrived. The man goes into the back and the store's lights go out. I see a telephone to one side. I'll call Granddad, and he'll come and get me.

"Can I use the phone?"

"Make it quick," the man says. He pulls on a heavy coat and jams a hat over the fringe.

I sift through my pockets and come up with a quarter.

"Is there a phone book?" I ask.

"Ed's not at the farm, if that's who you're calling."

Not at the farm? My heart plummets right to my feet. Shit! I didn't think for one minute that he wouldn't be here.

"Where is he?"

"Who's asking?"

"I'm his grandson, Dylan Wallace."

"Little Dylan." He looks me up and down. "Well, you sure sprouted up and up and up." He smiles at his own joke. "Ed used to bring you in here when you were small. Licorice."

"What?"

"It was licorice you always wanted. The red kind." He goes to a big jar on the counter and fishes out a string of red licorice and gives it to me.

Bewildered, I stand there holding it.

"Your granddad sure missed you when you went away. Especially after Anne died."

I hear my granddad calling to my grandmother. "Anne! Storm brewing." After he'd sniffed the air.

"Ed didn't know you were coming." It's not a question.

I shake my head.

"He's not at the farm any more. He's over at the Home. Been there most of the past year, but he's real bad now. He could go any minute. Lung cancer."

The shock must show in my face because the man claps me sympathetically on the shoulder.

"Guess you didn't know that. Come on. I'll give you a lift to the Home. They might not let you in, though. It's pretty late."

I follow him outside and into the cab of a pickup truck. The engine groans and protests the cold, then catches, and we move through a black-and-white world.

"Be up around your knees by morning."

"What?"

"The snow," he explains. "My name's Jack Cody." He sticks out a gloved hand and I shake it.

Murdock is a small town, one main street with a few others branching off it. Jack turns down one of the branches and stops in front of a long, low building with the name "Murdock Home" engraved on a plaque.

"Here it is," he says. "Miriam's on duty. She's a good sort. Just tell her who you are."

"Thanks," I say.

I wade through a snowdrift and walk up two steps to a set of double wooden doors. They're locked. I ring the bell and press my ear to the door, but I don't hear its shrill echo inside. I stab it again and hold my finger on it.

My ear is against the door when it swings open, and I nearly fall inside. A woman in a purple pantsuit glares at me.

"That bell is in perfectly fine working order," she says.

"Sorry. I'm looking for Edward Wallace."

"Not at this time of night you're not." She begins to shut the door.

"I'm his grandson. I've been on a bus all night to get here," I say desperately. "I didn't know he was sick."

The door swings wider. "Step in," she says. "You're letting all the heat out."

Actually, *she's* letting all the heat out, but I keep that observation to myself. I step inside to a hospital odour of bleach, pills, and illness. Miriam leads me down a dimly lit, tiled corridor to a small office. She shuts the door, turns on a lamp, and sits behind a desk. She gestures to a chair across from her and I'm in every principal's office I've ever been in. I automatically tense for a confrontation.

"So you're Ed's grandson," she begins.

"Dylan Wallace."

Sharp eyes take in every detail of me, and I cringe, wishing I'd had a good wash before I came. And brushed my teeth.

"You have the look of Ed about you," she says.

She gets up and leaves, returning a few minutes later with a steaming cup of chocolate that she places in front of me. "How long were you on the bus?"

"Five and a half hours." I sip the chocolate and feel its warmth slide down my throat.

"I'm Miriam Collins. I was in school with your mother," she says. "She was a couple years behind me. She left in grade ten." She flushes as she puts two and two together and figures out that I'm the reason Mom left school. "It's a small town. No secrets here. How is your mother?"

"Fine," I say. I toy with the idea of making up a great job for her, husband, family, but I'm too tired to work out all the details.

"You haven't seen your grandfather in a long time."

"Not for years," I say.

"You never got the letters he wrote to you?" she asks.

"I got one, just the other day." There were others? And how does this woman know about them?

The question must have been on my face because she smiles. "Like I said, it's a small town." Then the nurse in her takes over. "Your granddad has lung cancer," she continues briskly. "He's in the final stages. We're surprised he's still with us, but maybe there is a reason for that."

"What?" I ask dully. My brain can't process all this information.

"You," Miriam says. She stands. "Would you like to see him?"

I jump to my feet, but not to go see him. I want to leave, but it's real dark on the other side of the closed curtains and I have nowhere to spend the night. I follow Miriam down a second corridor and into a small room. It's full of shadows, and I can't see who is in the bed, though I hear a strange, uneven sighing, which I soon realize is breathing.

"You can sit here." Miriam takes my arm and steers me into a chair. She turns on a lamp on a night table that casts a small pool of light. "He's heavily sedated and on morphine for pain, but he wakes now and then," she says. "You don't have anywhere to go for the night?"

"No," I whisper. It's a place that discourages loud voices.

"You can stay here, then. If you need me, press this button." She points to a buzzer and cord attached to the bed with a large safety pin.

She leaves, and I immediately want to push the button, bring her back, and have her lead me out of this twilight world of near-death.

I listen to the breathing. It stops. Alarmed, I start from my chair, but with a gurgle, it begins again. After a long while, I get the nerve up to look at the man in the bed. Granddad.

No way! There is no way this shrunken, skeletal form beneath the sheet is my grandfather. Granddad was huge. The nurse has taken me to the wrong room. Over the bed is a small card with a name printed on it. I lean forward and read "Edward Wallace." I slump back in the chair and study him. Was he always this small? I know people shrink when they're old, but hell, he's barely a crease in the sheets! Maybe he was just big to a little kid. Maybe I needed him to be big. I still need him to be big. But he isn't.

Laying my head on the edge of the bed, I feel my tears wet the sheets. I must have fallen asleep, because I dream I feel the weight of a hand on my head, a large hand, and hear a voice whisper, "Dylan."

Chapter 19

A hand on my shoulder wakes me. At first, I think it's Grand-dad, and I raise my head quickly, but it's Miriam with a tray balanced on one hand.

"Merry Christmas," she says.

"Merry Christmas," I reply.

"You can use your grandfather's washroom to freshen up, and I brought you some breakfast." She sets the tray down on a table. "I'll be back soon."

I go into the washroom and find soap and have a wash. A quick look in a drawer reveals a half-used tube of toothpaste. I spend a long time brushing my teeth. It's been a while.

Breakfast is scrambled eggs, toast, juice, and milk, but, dis-appointingly, no coffee. I wolf the food down, pile the empty plates together, and then I have nothing to do.

A poinsettia sits on the windowsill. What idiot would send flowers to an unconscious man? I wander over, pick up the card tucked inside the leaves, and read, "From Myra and Jack." Jack—that would be the man in the store. As I put the card back, I feel vaguely ashamed.

Leaning over the Christmas plant, I pull the curtains open a crack and blink at the bright world outside. Snow powders each branch of a tree outside the window and glitters, diamond-brilliant. I leave the curtains open a slit and turn back to the room.

In the light from the window, I look at Granddad. Really look at him. His hair is still thick, though white now rather than the steel grey I remember. It sticks up in places, and I reach out a hand to smooth it. He stirs and his lips part. I wait, but no words come. With my forefinger, I touch the thin hand lying on the cotton sheet and feel skin like paper, bones brittle beneath, and remember the weight of a hand on my head. Was that real? His mouth is caved in slightly, and I realize his false teeth are out. I used to see those teeth in a glass by his bedside at the farm. They fascinated and repelled me. An uncomfortable-looking tube runs into his nose. Except for the hair, I can't find the grandfather I remember.

Miriam comes in and changes a bag on the intravenous stand.

"Are you sure this is Edward Wallace?" I ask.

"Of course this is Ed," she replies, surprised. "I've known Ed all my life." She glances at me. "You haven't seen him for a while, and you were just a little kid."

"Yeah, I guess that's it," I say. "He probably wouldn't recognize me."

"Oh, I don't know," she says. "We recognize the people we love no matter how much they change." She busies herself writing on a chart but keeps darting tiny glances at me.

"What?" I say finally.

"I guess you don't know this, but Phil is out at the farm," she says. "He arrived last week out of the blue."

"Sort of like me," I say, though my mind is in turmoil from her words.

"Sort of like you." She picks up the breakfast tray. "My

shift is over in an hour. If you want a ride out to the farm, I can give you one."

I can't say yes or no. Instead, I gesture toward the bed. "Can he hear anything?"

She creases her forehead. "I've heard of people regaining consciousness and saying that they've been aware of everything that went on around them. It certainly doesn't do any harm to talk to him. I'll be back in an hour."

I sink into a chair. So my father is at the farm. *Dad.* I try out the word and don't like it. I might joke about having three fathers, but I've never called anyone Dad.

I pull the Einstein book from my backpack and wonder how Twitch is doing. He, Amber, and Jenna seem so far away, in a completely different world. I open the book, but that's as far as I get. Miriam said I should talk to my grandfather, but I feel stupid chattering away to myself. My thoughts turn back to my father. Do I want to see him? He has never wanted to see me, so why would I want to see him? But I do.

If you stuff them too full, do brains explode? Mine is definitely going to. My head aches dreadfully. I force my mind to the book. *At the age of fifteen, Albert Einstein took an entrance exam to the Swiss Polytechnic, a university, attempting to bypass high school. He passed the technical portion but failed the arts exam.* Sort of overestimated yourself, didn't you, Einstein.

I leaf through the pages, and the words *black hole* catch my eye. *Einstein's Theory of Relativity describes the motions of bodies in strong gravitational fields at or near the speed of light. Though he did not believe in them himself, his work in physics is the basis for theory regarding black holes. It is believed that black holes form from the collapse of stars. The term "black hole" did*

*not come into being until after Einstein's death in 1955. Imagine
an object resting in the vast emptiness of space, totally unde-
tectable except for its gravitational pull. An object so massive,
and so densely packed, that no matter, communication, or even
light can escape its immense gravity.*

"Have you decided if you want to go to the farm?"

Miriam is back. I haven't decided, but I stand and pick up
my backpack.

"What a beautiful morning," Miriam exclaims as we head
out the door.

She's right. It is beautiful. It looks like every Christmas
card I've ever seen, blue sky above, clean, unbroken white
stretching before me. Jenna with her silver hair would fit in
perfectly here. Snow princess. Miriam and I tramp through
sculpted drifts to her car.

She drives carefully over snow-rutted roads. I try hard, but
I don't remember the town we pass through or the road
going to the farm.

"Did you know my mother's parents?" I ask.

"The Murrays? Sure."

"Do they still live here?"

Miriam nods. "A little ways out the other end of town. I
don't know them well. No one does. They keep to themselves.
They're"—she hesitates—"quite religious. Evangelical."

So Mom wasn't lying about that.

We drive in silence for a few minutes, Miriam concentrating on the icy road.

"The family is delaying Christmas until I get home," she
says. "The kids will be going crazy wanting to open their
presents, but I told them they had to wait."

More silence, then, "Do you have brothers or sisters?"

"Two brothers," I say shortly. I don't want to talk about them. Don't want to be reminded how much I miss them.

We turn down a second road, and Miriam stops at a snow-filled lane, a house attached to the end of it. "I'm not going down there—I might get stuck. But that's Ed's place," she says.

I look down the lane, and it's hard to breathe. I make no move to leave the car.

"You haven't seen your father for a long time, have you?"

"No." Never.

This is silly. Miriam has to get home so her kids can rip into their presents. I climb out of the car.

"Are you going to be okay?" she asks.

"Yeah. I'll be fine." I slam the car door shut. She does a careful U-turn and waves goodbye as she passes.

As I watch the car disappear down the lane, I realize I forgot to say thanks.

I heft my backpack onto my shoulders and trudge down the lane. Snow crunches beneath my running shoes, and Jack's prediction is correct. It's up to my knees. I glance behind me to see my footprints, the only indication of life in this white world. It's so quiet, it gives me the creeps. Halfway up the lane, I stop. A maple tree used to stand here. I'm so sure that I sweep aside snow with my foot and hit something hard. A stump. It makes me almost cheerful to know I was right.

The house looks smaller than I remember. I'm developing a theory that when you're a kid, everything appears twice as big as it really is. I must warn Micha so he's not devastated when he's older.

I climb ice-encrusted porch steps, slip, and grab a railing that wobbles alarmingly. A single rocking chair sits on the front porch, a forlorn sight.

It's so silent, I wonder if my father has left—the same way he came into town, without telling anyone. I'll probably leave that way myself. Who is there to say goodbye to?

I knock on the door and wait, but no one comes. Dropping my pack on the rocking chair, I go back down the icy steps. As I round the corner of the house, my feet falter, then stop altogether. Memories are everywhere. The yard, the barn, the vegetable garden, the bushes—brown and dead now, but forever green in my mind. This is where the fireflies flitted. And I know that really is my grandfather in the hospital bed. I've come too late. I catch my breath at the sudden pain in my chest. Heart-wrenching. That's a word I read once in a book. I didn't know what it meant at the time, but I do now.

A faint impression of tire tracks leads to a shed. I follow them and look through a window to see a rusted Ford inside. My father must still be here. Passing through the back porch, I knock on the door, then turn the knob. It's open.

"Hello," I call, as I walk into the kitchen.

The house is refrigerator cold, and my breath puffs white in front of me. I hear a crash, cursing, and a man staggers into the kitchen. My father. A stained T-shirt covers a flat belly, trousers unzipped beneath. He's shorter than me by nearly a head, but his arms are well muscled. His eyes are bloodshot and taking in the liquor and beer bottles on the counter, I wouldn't expect them to be otherwise. He's got Granddad's thick hair, but black. Like mine.

"Who the hell are you?" He glares at me and examines the bottles, shaking two. He flops into a chair with them in his hand.

"Well, whoever the hell you are—leave," he says. He drains a beer bottle.

"I'm Dylan."

He shakes the second bottle.

"Dylan Wallace," I say.

And, the wheels in his brain slowly start to turn. It's an effort, but he puts two and two together and comes up with—me. He upends the second bottle and drains it also.

"Hell. It's freezing in here." He stands and flaps his arms about his body. "The old man ran out of oil for the furnace. Bring in some wood."

Chapter 20

No *How are you, kid? Well, look at you.* He's been my father for all of three minutes and he's already ordering me about. At that moment, I decide to think of him as Phil, just another guy.

I get my pack from the rocking chair and find wood piled beneath the porch. Stacking logs and kindling in my arms, I go back into the house. I'm only doing this because I'm cold, too, not because he told me to. Cold in the city is bad, but out here it bites right through a person's clothes. Wadding up a newspaper, I stick it and kindling into the wood stove in the living room. I remember that black stove, heat kicking out from it and Grandma warning me not to get too close. It feels weird that I'm here and they aren't. It feels even weirder that Phil is. Flames leap up as the wood catches.

Phil comes down the stairs and passes into the kitchen without saying a word to me. He's pulled a navy blue cardigan over his T-shirt, one I remember as being Granddad's. It bothers me seeing it on him. I follow him into the kitchen, intent on finding food.

In the doorway, I stop abruptly. I was so shocked to see my father when I first walked in that I didn't take in the room.

The place is trashed. Bottles cover every surface. Dirty dishes are piled in the sink. A chair has been knocked over and left. A slow, burning anger begins in my stomach.

The floor sticks to my socks. I cross to the sink, open the cupboard beneath, and pull out dishwashing liquid. I turn taps and discover the water is still hot and fill the sink to soak the dishes.

"What are you, Little Susie Homemaker?" Phil asks.

Finding a box, I pile beer bottles in it.

"Anything in those?" He grabs one out of my hand and up-ends it. A small trickle hits the floor. I snatch it back, though I'm wary of those muscles in his arms.

"You got any money?" he asks.

"No," I say.

His eyes run up and down my frame. "Way you look, you got to be telling the truth."

He rummages in coat pockets and opens cupboard doors, pulling out cups and bowls. "I remember Ma used to squirrel money away in here for emergencies. And I guess we could call this an emergency. I'm out of beer," he says. From over the refrigerator, he pulls out a jar. "Here we go. You'd think the old man would have got rid of this." He unscrews the lid, pours out change onto the table, and counts. "Seven dollars," he says disgustedly. "Guess I can get a bottle of something." He scoops up the change and pulls on his coat.

"Stores are closed," I say.

"What?"

"The stores are closed. Liquor store, too."

He buttons up the jacket, unconvinced.

"It's Christmas Day," I tell him.

"Christmas Day? Shit!" He drops the coat onto the floor.

I make a show of picking it up and hanging it on a hook in the back porch.

"Quit doing that. You're making me nervous," he says.

"Grandma kept this place clean," I tell him.

He drops into a chair and lights up a cigarette. He doesn't offer me one. "Hey, you don't think I know that? They were my parents. I lived with them a lot longer than you did. Cleanliness is next to godliness. That was their motto."

"Then why are you being such a jerk and wrecking the place?" I ask.

He doesn't like that. I can see it in the squaring of his shoulders. He flicks ash onto the floor. "What are you doing here?"

"I came to see Granddad. What are you doing here?"

"I'm between jobs. I came back to the old homestead. Longing for hearth and home. You know how it is."

"I don't know," I say. "I never had a home. Just a lot of different houses and apartments." Let him make of that what he will.

I open the refrigerator. It's been cleaned out, but it still smells sour. I go into the porch and open the deep freeze. It, too, has been emptied.

"Anything in there?" Phil calls from the kitchen.

"No." I stand in the porch. Something's niggling at the back of my brain. Then I remember. When Grandma bought extra canned goods on sale, she'd put them on a shelf in the cupboard with the coats and boots. I look and, sure enough, there is a small stack of cans. I grab a chicken soup and go back into the kitchen.

"I'd forgotten about Ma putting stuff out there," Phil says when he sees the can in my hand.

I find an opener and look around for a pot. They're all filthy. I plunge one into the sink and scrub it, then empty the soup into it and place it on the stove. While it heats, I wash up the dishes, sitting them on the drainer to dry.

"Well, aren't you responsible," Phil says. "Dad must have loved you."

Did Granddad love me? If so, why didn't he try harder to find me?

"The old man was always after me to be more responsible. Do your chores. Do your school work. That's all he ever thought about, work, work, work." He drops his cigarette butt in a beer can and immediately lights another. "Who needs that crap all the time?"

From the window over the sink, I see dark menacing clouds gathering on the horizon. More snow.

"We don't have a freezer," I say.

"What?"

"We don't have a freezer. We don't have enough food to eat, let alone any extra to freeze."

"Hey, that's not my fault," Phil says. "It was your mother's decision to have you. It had nothing to do with me. She could have got rid of you. Then we wouldn't be having this conversation, would we?"

Ignoring him, I pour a bowl of soup for myself and sit in Grandma's rocking chair near the wood stove. From the kitchen, I hear the pot scrape across the burner, and a moment later Phil comes in with the pot and a spoon. He sits in my granddad's chair.

Soup finished, I wander around the room and find a duplicate of the wedding picture I have tucked away in my Einstein book. There are other pictures, too, of women in long dresses and men in starched collars, all solemn. Picture-taking must have been a serious business back then.

On a hutch among teacups and saucers, I find a photo of myself. I'm about three years old, standing beside my granddad next to the old maple tree in the lane. In the picture, I'm grinning from ear to ear. I can't remember ever being so happy that I'd smile that widely. Granddad's hand rests on my head, and I feel again the weight of the hand in the hospital.

"So how's your mother doing?" The soup seems to have thawed Phil slightly.

"She's fine," I say shortly.

"You go to school?"

"Not at the moment."

"I didn't have much time for school, either. I learned more from the school of life." He lights a cigarette. "Guess I better go easy on these, seeing as it's Christmas Day. They'll have to last me until tomorrow."

"What do you do?" I ask. "When you're not between jobs."

"A little bit of everything. Last job, I was unloading ships in Halifax. I got tired of it, though. It's hard work."

"Have you been to the Home to see Granddad?" I ask.

"Stopped by on my way through town. Wasn't much point, though. He didn't even know I was there. All my going did was get the tongues wagging in town."

He flicks ash on the carpet.

"Don't do that," I say.

"What?"

"The floor. It's not an ashtray."

Phil tips back his chair. "Who gives a shit? The old man is

never going to see this place again. Besides, it'll be mine shortly. So I guess I can do what I want with it," he continues.

"Yeah, well, it's not yours yet," I tell him.

I go into the kitchen, find a pail, fill it with hot water, and plunge a beat-up mop into it. Pushing chairs out of the way, I tackle the floor. I need to do something because my hands are itching to punch and pound.

The floor is done, and suddenly, so I am. I'm so tired I can barely stand. I grab my pack and head upstairs.

The stove's heat doesn't reach here, but I fill the bathtub with hot water and climb in. After a long soak, I wrap myself in a towel and go into Grandma and Granddad's bedroom. I thought my father might be sleeping in there, but the comforter on the bed is undisturbed. I slip between sheets that feel cold and slightly damp, but I settle into the slight depression in the mattress where Granddad used to lie, and my eyes close.

When I wake, shadows fill the room. I pull on my clothes and go to the window. Snow falls, thick and silent, shutting me off from the world. It puts me on edge, the snow and the approaching dark.

From downstairs I hear doors slam and the sound of breaking glass. Heart beating rapidly, I grab my pack and head toward the noise. The living room is cold again, Phil not bothering to add wood to the stove. He's going through the buffet and hutch, roughly shoving things aside. I hear the tinkle of breaking china.

"Nothing!" He slams a door shut with a crash. "He wouldn't have a drop in the house." He sweeps a hand across the buffet top and the wedding picture goes flying. Face red, he stamps across the carpet and steps on the picture, glass crunching beneath his heel.

My anger boils over. I flail at him with my fists, but he easily backs out of my reach. He's obviously practised at fighting.

"What the hell's your problem?"

I come at him again. "You're an asshole! A fucking asshole. No wonder Granddad hated you. I hate you. I'd rather be like him than you any day." I connect with his chin and he staggers back.

I have time to see the surprise in his eyes, then I'm flat on my back from a blow to the side of my face. For a few minutes, the room spins crazily. He stands over me, breathing hard, and I fold into myself, expecting another punch. But it doesn't come. He backs away.

"Not like me? Look at yourself. You're a loser. Just like me. I don't give a shit about your lousy life," he shouts. "If you came here looking for a father, you won't find one. You're nothing to me. You understand? Nothing!"

Chapter 21

Dragging my pack behind me, I stumble through the kitchen to the porch. As I pull on my coat, I see car keys sitting on the freezer. It's a long way to town, too far to walk in the dark and cold. I snatch up the keys and go outside. A brisk wind pushes snow in my face as I run across the yard to the shed. The doors are frozen shut, but I lean on them and they open. I glance quickly over my shoulder, but I don't see Phil coming after me. Throwing my pack into the passenger side of the car, I slide into the driver's seat. My hands shake, but I fit the key in the ignition and turn it.

The car roars into life. In the rear-view mirror, I see a shadow at the porch window, then a square of yellow light falls across the yard as the back door opens. I ram the gearshift to "R" and push the accelerator to the floor. I've never driven before, but how hard can it be? As the car shoots out of the garage on an angle, the rear bumper takes out one of the shed doors.

Phil sprints toward the shed, hands waving, mouth open, but I have the engine roaring so loudly I can't hear him. I can imagine what he's saying, though. Frantically, I shove the gear into drive. Wheels spin uselessly, and Phil looms out of the dark and grabs the passenger door handle. Suddenly, the tires catch and I plow forward through drifts. Phil leaps back and sprawls in the snow. The car swerves from side to side as I drive down what I think is the lane. It's hard to tell, because I can't find the headlights. But nothing stops my progress, like a tree or fence, so I keep my foot on the accelerator. The windshield fogs up inside and I rub my hand across it, but that just smears the wet. I can't see a thing. I catch a glimpse of the mailbox and realize I'm at the road, and I turn sharply to the left.

My eyes dart back and forth between the windshield and the various levers on each side of the steering wheel. I push and pull at them, and finally headlights come on and wipers sweep across the windshield. It doesn't help, as the snow is coming down diagonally, cutting my visibility to zero. The back of the car fishtails, and I raise my foot slightly from the gas. The sign for the main road leaps out of the dark. I slam my foot down on the brake, but the car doesn't stop. It skids sideways, across the road and into a ditch.

Okay, so driving is not as easy as it looks. I sit, the breath knocked out of me by the steering wheel hitting my chest. After a few minutes, I put the car in reverse and try to back out of the ditch, but it's too deep. I'm not going anywhere. I turn off the engine and run through my options: return to the farm and my father, which is certain death, or walk through the snow and dark into town, which is also certain death. Some choice. But I'd rather take death by freezing than a beating, so I decide to walk.

Leaving the keys in the ignition for Phil to find, I grab my backpack and climb out of the car. I scramble up the steep side of the ditch and stand on the road, disoriented. The curtain of snow parts briefly and I see a faint orange glow in the sky to the west, so I head in that direction.

My face hurts like hell where my father hit me and I scoop up snow to put against my cheek. I'm shivering already, though I've walked only twenty steps from the car. Who am I kidding? I'll never make it to town. They'll find my stiff, frozen body by the side of the road.

So how was your Christmas, Dylan? Super. The best fucking Christmas ever. I sat in a hospital with a dying man, and then I met and fought my moron father. There was no heat, no turkey, no tree, no gifts, and now I'm walking through the frozen wilderness. I have a theory, which my experiences have proven, that when you're down, life takes a giant boot and stomps on you for good measure.

From the road behind me, I hear the sound of an approaching car engine. I'm getting ready to dive into the ditch when a pickup pulls up beside me, a window rolls down, and Jack sticks his head out.

"What the hell are you doing out here?" he asks.

"Walking to town," I reply.

"Get in."

I climb into the pickup.

"Would you know anything about that car back there in the ditch?" he asks.

I shrug and hold my frozen hands to the vent in the dashboard. It's painful, but it feels great.

"Someone will find it. I take it you were at the farm. Is Phil still there?"

He's just full of questions.

He throws a glance at my damaged face, then back to the road. "Appears the reunion didn't go too well."

He squints and slows the pickup as a gust of wind-blown snow obliterates the road in front of us. "Helluva night to be out. Lucky for you I came along. Burglar alarm went in the store. I expect it's just the storm setting it off. Still, I have to check."

We pass a cluster of houses and then we're in the town itself. "Where are you going?" he asks.

"I'm catching the next bus that comes through," I tell him. "I have a return ticket."

"There's nothing until eleven tomorrow morning," Jack says.

"Oh." In the city, buses and trains run day and night. I guess I'll find a doorway, wrap myself inside my sleeping bag, and wait for morning. That will be a novelty for this town. I bet they don't have street kids here.

"I could take you back to the Home," Jack suggests.

"Fine." I don't want to go back there, but at least it'll be warm.

This time, Jack parks the pickup and comes to the door of the Home with me. I expect to see Miriam, but it's a different nurse on duty, younger, with black hair pulled into a ponytail. Jack steps in with me, takes her to one side for a brief chat, and comes back.

"It's been real nice seeing you again, Dylan." He pulls off his glove and sticks out his hand. "You ever need anything, you let me know. Ed's a good friend of mine, and I'd consider it an honour to help one of his people."

I take the offered hand and shake it. He really seems to mean it.

"I'm sorry about this." He points to my face. "That's Phil. But you should know that your grandfather—well, he cared about you, boy," he says quickly. "Talked about you all the time. Said he was going to start a court case to get custody of you."

"Why didn't he?" I ask. I feel like Grandma's china, broken into small pieces.

"He started the proceedings, but it takes a long time. Anne got ill, and died, and it took the life right out of him," Jack says. "Then those letters he sent to you—most came back unopened. He thought he'd lost you. By then, he was ill himself."

I want to believe him. I really do. But I've been crapped on so many times.

"Anyway, you take care of yourself." Jack nods at the nurse and leaves.

"I'm Amy," the girl says. "You look like you could do with a bit of food inside you."

She walks briskly down the corridor. Most of the rooms we pass are lit and filled with people visiting for Christmas. Granddad's room is dark.

"Here we are." She turns on the lamp. "You get cleaned up a bit, and I think I can find a turkey dinner for you."

I go into the washroom and let hot water run over my hands. I splash it onto my face, wincing when it hits my sore cheek.

Back in the room, I sit in the chair beside the bed. Nothing's changed. Granddad's hands lie unmoving on the white sheet, his mouth is slightly open, his breathing erratic. There are voices in the corridor as people walk by, glance in, and go on, and suddenly, I'm glad I'm here. Fiercely glad I am with Granddad. On Christmas night.

Amy returns with a tray piled with covered plates that she sets on the table. "Here you go."

Turkey, dressing, mashed potatoes, cranberry sauce, carrots and peas, and pie for dessert. It smells wonderful. I dig in as she tucks a sheet around Granddad.

"You can press charges, if you like," she says.

Puzzled, I look up from the food.

"Assault charges."

"Oh." I shake my head.

She gently fixes the pillow behind my grandfather's head. "Ed's a lovely man," she says. "Real nice."

"He used to take me out and show me fireflies," I tell her.

"Did he? That's great."

Why did I tell her that? Tears sting behind my eyes.

"I'll bring you some ice for your cheek," Amy says.

And I'm left alone with my turkey dinner and Granddad.

Scraping the last morsel of mashed potato from the plate, I push the tray away and stare at the man in the bed. Lovely, Amy said. And nice. Miriam said I had the look of him about me. To hell with Phil.

I sit in the chair and doze, wake, and hear the quiet all around me, so I know it's late. Someone—Amy, I guess—has turned out the light, so I cross to the window and open the curtains to see that the sky has cleared and blue moon shadows stretch across the snow. I leave the curtains open, letting the moonlight fall across Granddad. I think he'd like that. Then, suddenly, I reach out and wrap my granddad's hand in mine, like he once held mine, and for a while, the anger inside me quiets.

Then it's morning. Amy brings me breakfast and says she's off duty soon and will give me a ride to the store.

I wander around the room, waiting for her, feeling antsy.

"Ready to go?" She hands me a scarf, gloves, and a hat with earflaps. "These were your grandfather's," she says, almost apologetically. "Not the height of fashion, but they will keep you warm. I noticed you didn't have any last night."

"Thanks." I pull on the hat, catch my reflection in the mirror, and it's sort of cool. I like that it was his.

"Do you have anywhere you can be reached for . . . well . . . you know." She gestures toward the bed.

I begin to shake my head, when I remember Glen's card. "You can reach me here. He's a . . ." What is he? "A friend of mine." I guess. I read the number to her and she jots it down.

Before we leave, I look at the bed once more, the shrunken figure. And I wait. Because if this were television, Granddad would suddenly open his eyes, beckon me close, and in a gasping voice say, "Dylan," or something profound. But the eyes remain closed, the lips don't form words, and the breathing rattles. This isn't television.

Chapter 22

Land stretches out from the bus window in gentle swells. Earlier in the day, the wind changed direction from north to south, melting the snow to reveal brown patches of plowed fields. The highway is deserted. The bus is deserted. I'm exhausted, but my brain won't stop spinning. Murdock. My father. Granddad. Dying. Jenna. And me.

What am I going back to? Absolutely nothing.

In the gloom of late afternoon, we come into the city, past apartments, townhouses, and streets of identically built box-like houses. Through lighted windows, I catch glimpses of ordinary people, ordinary lives—a table set for dinner, the flicker of a television screen. At least it's what I think ordinary is.

It's nearly dark when I step off the bus. The streets are rain-slick and quiet. People from the bus hurry away to family, to friends, to people who care. I'm alone. Three days ago, I thought everything would be different.

There's only one place I can think to go, the donut shop, the nearest thing to a home I have now. I jump over a pile of brown slush at the curb, remember the white blanket over the farm, and trudge the three blocks to Mandy's.

It's full of people like me, losers with nowhere else to go

on the day after Christmas. Three goth chicks cluster around a table in the middle of the room, a black blemish against the garish red and yellow of the shop's walls. They laugh and exhale blue smoke into the air, despite the No Smoking signs. Lurch holds court with the four Bandana Kids in the far corner, no doubt impressing them with his baddest-of-the-bad routine. I debate leaving to avoid trouble, but I'm too tired. Besides, trouble will find me no matter where I go. The Garbage Man sits in a booth at the back, eyes darting fearfully between Lurch and the door. The Swear Lady, swaddled in clothing, sits beside her cart, muttering non-stop. The waitress leans sleepily on the counter, brown visor askew.

Ainsley is in a booth with Amber, coffee cups between them. She's leaning forward, speaking earnestly, and Amber shrinks against the vinyl backrest, looking uncomfortable. A quick scan of the room turns up no Jenna. And no Twitch.

I thread my way between tables to Ainsley's booth. She stops talking and leans back.

Amber greets me happily. "Hi, Dylan. How's it going?" She doesn't wait for an answer but manipulates her bulk out of the booth, taking the opportunity to escape Ainsley. When she stands, I'm amazed to see how huge her stomach is.

"Thanks for the coffee, Ainsley," she says, and wanders over to Lurch.

"Did I interrupt something?" I ask.

"Coffee," Ainsley says disgustedly. "She should be drinking milk." She smiles at me wearily. "I was trying to convince her to see the street nurse. She's not had any prenatal care at all. And look at her!" She gestures toward Amber. "Skin and bones."

I raise my eyebrows. "She looks pretty big to me."

"That's just baby," Ainsley explains. "She's malnour-
ished, which means the baby isn't getting the proper nutri-
tion, either."

"Vulture cut her loose. She's got no money for food."

"Who's Vulture?" Ainsley asks.

"Oh, that's my name for Brendan," I say sheepishly.

"Vulture." Ainsley smiles into her coffee cup. "Can I get
you something to drink, Dylan?"

"I'm good." I am thirsty, but I don't want to be obligated.

"How did your trip go?"

I raise my eyebrows. "Are you playing social worker?" I
ask. "First with Amber and now me?"

"Don't be a jerk," she says, but there's no anger in her
voice. "Glen told me that you were going to see your grandfather."

I don't like Glen spreading my business around. What else
has he told her?

I slide into the booth. "My grandfather's dying from lung
cancer, my father's an asshole, the farm's trashed, Murdock's
waist-deep in snow. You know how it is."

"I'm sorry," Ainsley says.

I shrug.

"What happened to your face?"

"Christmas gift from my father."

"Oh. So what are you going to do next?" she asks.

My mouth drops open in astonishment. It's not like I have
a ton of options!

"I know," Ainsley continues. "Life just dumped on you
again. You can wallow around in that some, but you can't
change it. It's history. So, it's time to look ahead. What are
you going to do now?"

"What can I do?" I don't believe her.

"Start with something small, like tonight. You need a place to sleep. I can arrange something for you at a shelter, and then you can—"

I don't want to hear this. "Where's . . ." I want to say Jenna, but instead ask, "Where's Twitch?"

Ainsley stirs her coffee. "In the hospital. He's sick with pneumonia and hepatitis. They're not sure if he's going to pull through."

She lets me digest that, then goes on. "If he does pull through, he'll be a long time getting better. Then he'll go into rehab. And then he'll be right back out here on the streets, starting all over again. He doesn't have a hope in hell. He's illiterate. He'll start dealing again. Using. It's a vicious circle. He'll never break free of it."

"But you did," I say.

"With help," she says. "There's still a chance for you, Dylan, but you don't have to do it yourself. That's what I'm trying to offer you here, help. I'm not telling you what to do. You have to decide that yourself. But I can suggest routes to take to make it a bit easier."

Before she can say more, a car sweeps into the parking lot and screeches to a stop in front of the window. The passenger door opens and Jenna gets out. She strolls over to the driver's side, leans in the window a moment, then steps back as the car takes off with a squeal of wheels.

I grab my pack. "See you around," I say to Ainsley, but my eyes never leave Jenna.

"Dylan . . ." Ainsley reaches out to stop me, but I'm halfway to the door.

Jenna walks across the parking lot and stands beneath a light standard, head bent, looking at something in her hands.

Anger surges through me as I push the door open and stride over to her. "Hey," I yell.

Startled, she turns, her hands going behind her back.

"What do you have there?" I ask.

I grab her arm and wrench it in front and pry her fingers open to find a folded wad of bills.

"Turning tricks. You're turning tricks!"

"It's none of your business what I do," she says.

"You said you were going to meet me at the bus station. I waited. You didn't show."

"Something came up."

She begins to go around me, but I grab her arm and force her back to face me.

"I told you he'd have you on the streets, didn't I? Your precious Brendan."

She pulls her arm free. "I have food in my stomach and a bed. It's a job."

"You're a whore," I tell her. "Look at you. Skirt up to your ass. You're a whore."

"Don't do this, Dylan. Please." She puts a hand out to push me away, but I grab it and pin her to my body.

"Why don't you do me, whore? You're doing everyone else. Why not me?"

"Let go," she screams. She places both hands on my chest and shoves. I stagger back and my arms fall away.

She begins to cry. "Why did you do that?"

"Because you're out there fucking men for money." I hate that men touch her: her hair, her lips, her breasts.

She dashes away the tears. "It's not like I've never done this before," she says. "And there was no money involved then. He said it was for love. Love."

Tears stream down her face.

"Who said? Brendan? Who?" I don't get it.

Her eyes suddenly widen with alarm. She puts her face next to mine and whispers urgently in my ear, "Lurch is coming over. Get out of here. Brendan knows that you asked me to go away with you. He's out to get you."

"How would he know that?" I ask. Though there's really only one answer.

"I had to tell him. You don't understand. Just leave, before you get hurt."

She steps away, pushes at me again with both hands, and laughs loudly. "Come back when you're a grown man." She gaily waves the bills at Lurch, takes his arm, and pulls him back toward the donut shop, but his eyes lock with mine as he lets himself be led away.

Leave, she told me, but where is there to go? There is the abandoned factory, with the psychos in the shadows, or the men's shelter, where the weirdos are out in plain view.

It's going to be a long night. I dig Granddad's hat out of my pack and put it on my head and begin to walk. A cop car slows beside me, a window rolls down, and a head sticks out. Then abruptly the window closes, the lights flash on top, and the siren wails as the car speeds away. Obviously more important events needing his attention than a street kid. Shit. I don't even matter to the cops!

I have an unformed hope that Holy Rosary might be open. A sanctuary. I could camp out on a hard wooden pew. But I arrive to find a padlock securing the gate. I turn away, and there they are. Surrounding me, Lurch and the four Bandana Kids. I never even heard them come up.

Without a word, Lurch steps forward and hits me in the stomach with a fist. Pain rips through my abdomen. My breath whooshes out as I double over. Another blow catches me on the back of the neck and agony explodes in my head as I go down. Hard cement grazes my cheek, but that is the least of the pain. Boots catch me in the ribs. I hear a distinct crack. Fists plow into my kidneys, nose, and split my lips. Non-stop blows and kicks. I feel a tug at my arms and I realize they are after my backpack. I begin to fight back with my fists, feet, arms, teeth, but there are too many of them. Voices shout, fade, and my pack is gone. There's no point in fighting any more. I let myself sink into blackness. They've taken my entire life. They've taken—me.

Chapter 23

Hands claw at my arms. Pulling, tugging, all to the accompaniment of a steady string of profanity.

"Leave me alone," I mumble. I hurt. Everywhere. Badly. I want back into that cocoon of darkness where no pain exists.

But the fingers continue running up and down my arms, my legs, prodding my ribs. I force open swollen eyes to see the Swear Lady bending over me. Breath foul, she curses non-stop, and I realize, in between obscenities, she's asking me, am I okay? Can I move my legs?

"Oh God! Dylan!" Jenna kneels down beside me. Silver hair gleams like a halo. Guess I'm dead, but I don't mind if there are angels like Jenna.

From behind her, Amber's face swims into view. "Oh, fuck," she says. No angel. I'm not dead.

The Swear Lady talks in her weird mixture of the obscene and normal, and Amber turns to me. "Gladdy thinks your ribs are broken."

"Gladdy?" I croak.

Amber nods toward the Swear Lady. "Her. Gladdy."

The Swear Lady has a name?

"She used to be a nurse, before . . ." Amber stops, at a loss for words.

Before her brain got hot-wired.

"You need to go to the hospital," Amber continues.

"No," I reply thickly.

Tears stream down Jenna's face. "This is all my fault. I'm so sorry, Dylan." She looks wildly up and down the street. "What should we do? What if they come back?"

"Factory," I whisper.

"What?" Jenna says.

"There's an abandoned factory some of us are staying at, but he'll never walk that far," Amber tells her.

I try to climb to my feet, but fall back and whimper.

"Would you stop being a fucking hero?" Amber puts my arm around her shoulder and tries to heave me up. "You need a hospital."

"No."

"Fucking idiot," Amber says. "Would you help here?" she yells at Jenna.

Jenna takes my other arm, and between the two of them, they pull me to my feet. I grab the shopping cart to steady myself, and the Swear Lady starts to scream and hit at my hands. I understand why. Her life is in there. My life was in my backpack.

"Gladdy," Amber explains patiently, "he only needs to use it to hold himself up. Like a walker, like old people use? He won't take it."

Gladdy doesn't look convinced, but the wailing subsides. Grudgingly, she lets me hold onto the cart, though she hangs on to the handle as we start off.

It's a nightmare journey with nightmare characters. Me staggering behind a shopping cart, Gladdy bundled in her clothes, swearing under her breath, Amber heavy with her baby, Jenna crying.

I'm not sure how I crawl through the fence at the factory or get up the iron stairs. But somehow I do. A fire is lit, but the people around it melt away when they see my broken body.

I shake uncontrollably, which causes excruciating pain in my chest. "Sleeping bag," I say between shudders.

"It's gone," Jenna says, and she begins to cry again.

"Stop that fucking noise," Amber says to her. "Do something useful. Find some more wood for the fire."

"Fire's dangerous," I whisper.

"You need to be warm," Amber says.

Jenna hurries away and brings back an armful of wooden slats. Amber heaps them onto the fire and it flares brightly. She finds an old blanket and begins to lay me down, but I scream from the pain, feel the room spin, myself leaving my body.

"Shit! No. No." Gladdy sits me up again and tells Amber to find something for me to lean against.

The girl disappears into the shadows and comes back lugging a lopsided ottoman. Gladdy gently leans me against it. I still hurt, but I can at least breathe now.

Gladdy explains to Amber about broken ribs, how a person can't lie flat. Through my pain, I marvel at the part of her brain that remembers being a nurse. Then, abruptly, Gladdy breaks off talking and sniffs the air. *Storm brewing, Annie.* Gladdy takes her cart and shuffles off into the dark.

A moment later, Vulture steps into the circle of firelight, two of the Bandana Kids behind him. "So what happened here?" he asks.

"Shut the fuck up," Amber says.

"Better watch your mouth, bitch," Vulture tells her. "I heard there was a fight. I came to find out how the boy is doing."

Amber gets to her feet. "Yeah, you're a real fucking sweetheart."

Vulture crouches down beside me. "Nice place. I can see why you'd rather live here than work for me." He tilts his head to one side and studies me. "Hurting, are you?"

"Fuck off," I say.

Vulture laughs, gets to his feet, and grabs Jenna's arm. "What the hell are you doing here?" He gives her a shake.

"I'm just . . ." she stutters. "I was leaving soon."

He pushes her away, and she falls to her knees. "You better be leaving real soon." He walks out of the firelight, and footsteps ring on the iron staircase.

Jenna picks herself up. Tears stream down her face.

"Go home," I tell her.

She shakes her head, plunges a hand into her coat pocket, and brings out two white pills.

"Take these. They'll help the pain."

She pushes the tablets into my mouth, and I choke them down.

"See you later," she says, and hurries away.

Then it's just Amber and me and the people in the shadows.

"He is such a fucking asshole," Amber says. She tugs at the hat on my head. "You'll be more comfortable with this off."

"No. Leave it." The words burst from me, surprising her. Surprising me.

"Okay, okay." Amber puts the hat back on my head. "Dylan, I have to go and get some things. I'll be back as soon as I can."

I grab her hand and hold tight, terrified of being left alone, but she gently pries my fingers off. "I promise I'll come back."

After a while, the pills take effect and the pain loosens its clutch on me. A figure detaches itself from the shadows, throws a couple pieces of wood on the dying fire, and disappears so quickly I can't tell who it is. But I think I hear the swishing of garbage bags.

Mesmerized, I watch flames leap and coil, taking on fantastic shapes of animals and birds, distorted stone gargoyles with lips stretched unimaginably large, leering at me. Hideous, they grow up into the dark reaches of the factory ceiling and I cower from them. Eventually, this, too, passes, and my eyes close.

I wake to pain and cold. Amber is beside me, holding a cup to my lips. Hot coffee. I try to sip, but it stings my torn lips and I jerk my head away. That brings on the pain in my chest and, well, everywhere else. I gasp and cry, hear myself and feel ashamed, but I can't stop. I've never hurt so much in my life. Not even after Pete got through with me.

"Pills. Jenna," I croak.

Amber hesitates, then reaches into her pocket and pulls out two of the white pills. "She left these for you." Eagerly, I swallow them.

Amber opens a box of baby wipes and gently cleans my face.

"You really do need a fucking doctor or something," she says, biting back tears. Amber crying scares me. She's tough, so I must be really bad.

The pills take effect, and I relax slightly. I move a hand and discover it's under a blanket. I gesture toward the coffee cup and Amber holds it to my lips again. This time I'm able to drink a bit of the liquid, feel it burn down my throat. Then I have to pee. Something fierce.

I struggle to get to my feet.

"What are you doing?" Amber asks, alarmed.

"Toilet."

She hauls me to my feet and into a corner, and turns her back while I do my business. Finished, I wrap an arm around her shoulder and stagger back to the ottoman. She lowers me down, then collapses beside me. "You're fucking heavy," she says. She tucks the blanket around both of us.

"You're so beautiful," I tell her.

"I look like shit," Amber says. "That's just the pills talking. Besides, it's Jenna you like, remember?"

Jenna. But it's Amber who is here, taking care of me.

For days, I drift in a drugged fog. The fire is lit at night. Someone helps me up to the john in the corner when I need it. My ribs get poked and my shirt comes off and a cloth is wrapped tightly around my chest, accompanied by the most profane language I've ever heard. Jenna comes and pushes pills into my mouth. I hear her argue with Amber.

"Those aren't going to help," Amber shouts. "Do you think I'm a fucking idiot? I know who's behind this."

"They make him feel better," Jenna says, and disappears into the shadows.

"Stupid bitch!" Amber yells after her.

I open my eyes and Ainsley is crouched beside me. "You can press charges if you want, but you'll have to go to a doctor and the police." She tells me this half-heartedly, knowing I won't report the beating. Her head looms monstrous in front of mine. I cringe back.

"What is he on?" she asks Amber.

"I don't know. Jenna keeps bringing him pills."

"Shit," Ainsley says. "He's so high. Look, Dylan. You need food and warmth and proper care. Otherwise, you'll be in the hospital with Twitch."

Twitch. Obviously still alive or she would have said "in the ground with Twitch." In the cold, cold grave with Twitch. I giggle.

"Jenna says your ribs are broken." Ainsley unbuttons my coat, pulls up my shirt, and gently touches the bandage.

"Who did this?" she asks. "It looks pretty good."

"Gladdy," Amber says.

Ainsley pulls the shirt down and tucks the blanket around me. "You can't keep taking those pills, Dylan," she says.

Yes, I can, because they stop the pain, in my body and in my mind.

Ainsley drifts away.

The reality is, the pills do stop the pain, but only for a while, and that while is becoming shorter and shorter before the hurting comes back, along with a black despair that only Jenna and her magic tablets can take away.

One night, I wake and Amber gives me a sip of water, then settles beside me under the blanket. "I want a smoke so fucking bad," she says. "But I'm trying to cut back for the baby. Gladdy says I should."

"How do you know her name?"

"She told me. I didn't ask her," she adds hastily.

"The Garbage Man?"

"The garbage man . . ." Amber shakes her head, puzzled, then her face clears. "Oh, you mean Paul."

"Paul," I repeat. "Do you know everyone's name?"

"No. Just the ones who tell me when we're talking."

I mull that over. Amber treats everyone out here like normal people, not homeless street losers, and in return they give her their names.

"What's your name?" I ask.

"You know who I am."

"Your real name," I say.

She's quiet a moment. "Faith," she says eventually.

"Your name is Faith?"

"That's what my momma named me."

"Where is she? Your mother?"

"Dead. She was a junkie. Out on the streets, just like me. I guess the apple doesn't fall far from the tree. I lived in care until I was fourteen, then I ran away. My momma loved me, but the drugs . . . I guess she loved them more.

"Feel this." Amber places my hand on her stomach and I feel movement beneath my fingers. "It's the baby," she says.

"Is it creepy having a human inside you?" I ask.

"Of course it's not creepy, you fucking idiot." She sounds indignant. "It's my baby. Men, you're all so fucking stupid."

"Guess what your baby's first word will be."

Amber settles back down and gives me a tiny punch. "Yeah, I know. I'll clean up my mouth after it's born. Everything will be different after the baby's born."

Chapter 24

One day, Jenna doesn't come with her pills. All night I tremble, cold and hot, and cower from fearsome creatures just beyond the fire's light. Amber crawls under the blanket and wraps her arms around me.

"I'm dying," I tell her.

"You're just coming down," she assures me. "You'll feel better when the drugs get out of your body."

I push her away and roll into a tight ball.

Morning comes and I drag myself to my feet and stand, swaying, shocked that I am so weak. Forcing my legs to move, I step over a sleeping Amber and shuffle to the iron stairs. Already, my T-shirt is damp and stinking from the effort. The crawl through the hole in the fence nearly does me in, but after a short rest, I stumble away from the factory. On a quest for the magic pills.

Frost rimes every branch, white lace against a cobalt blue sky. My breath puffs in clouds that hang in the air, no wind to carry them away. My fingers burn from the cold. My gloves were in my backpack.

I have no idea what day it is or how long I was in the factory. The streets are quiet. Occasionally, a person scurries past, collar clutched tight against the cold. They give me wide berth, and catching my reflection in a window, I know why. Even in this makeshift mirror I can see the swelling around my eyes, a spreading bruise on my cheek. Granddad's cap is pulled low over my forehead.

As I step away from the window, my legs give out, and I stagger and lean against a concrete wall, breathing shallowly against the intense pain in my chest. A man walks by, an iced pastry at his mouth. When did I eat last? As he passes a trash bin, he tosses the half-eaten Danish into it. There it sits, right on top. I shuffle over to the can, grab the pastry, and shove it into my mouth. As I chew, I dig through the garbage to see if there's anything else to eat. Hair rises on the back of my neck, and with a spurt of fear I swing around. A woman stands behind me, face twisted in disgust. She's stout, obviously hasn't missed many meals, so I give her the finger and she hurries away. I continue to root in the garbage bin. I'm now a dumpster diver.

Up and down the streets I weave like a drunk, searching. I avoid the youth centre, the office tower, and street school. Finally, I find what I've been looking for. One of the Bandana Kids stands outside a video arcade, having a smoke. When I first approach him, he tenses, but he relaxes when he sees my unsteady steps.

"You don't look so hot, man," he says finally.

"Yeah," I mumble, lips still swollen. It's like I'm trying to talk through someone else's mouth. I don't point out the obvious to him. He did this to me.

He flicks ash away and waits.

"You got anything?" I ask.

"What are you looking for?"

I stamp numb feet, then wish I hadn't as pain courses through my body. How can a person hurt so much? "Painkillers."

"That might be possible." He grinds the butt beneath his boot. "Meet me here, seven tonight," he says.

"Do you have anything now?" I ask. It's grovelling, but I'm desperate.

He checks up and down the street, then reaches into a back pocket and extracts a single pill. "That should hold you until tonight," he says. "See you at seven."

"I haven't got any money . . ." I begin.

"At seven," he repeats, and goes back into the arcade.

I down the pill quickly, then force my brain to think. The factory is too far to walk back to, but I can't stay any longer in the cold. The closest place is the library.

Somehow, I get my broken body past the security guard and into a chair in the library lounge. My hand automatically reaches out to wrap the strap of my backpack around my ankle, but there's nothing there. I miss my life that was inside: the Einstein book Twitch gave me, the gloves, my dirty clothes, the CD player from Glen—the only gift I got this Christmas—and Grandma and Granddad's wedding picture. The pill kicks in and I spend the afternoon staring at nothing.

At ten to five, I ease myself from the chair and make a bee-line for the washroom. As I push open the door, I stop in my tracks at the sight of a filthy man, eyes swollen half shut, face bruised yellow and purple, ridiculous hat pulled low over his forehead and ears. It takes a minute to recognize the person in the mirror as me. I study my beaten face, and a tear squeezes out of a blackened eye and runs down my cheek.

Outside, my legs, stiff from sitting all afternoon, will barely move. It's colder than before and my shivering hurts my ribs. I need those pills.

As I walk past Holy Rosary Cathedral, I see Glen coming toward me, a briefcase in his hand. I consider turning around and hurrying the other way but immediately discard that idea. I couldn't hurry if I tried.

He draws level, stops, and stares at my face. "Ainsley said you looked bad, but her description didn't do you justice. That's quite a beating you took."

I shrug.

"Dylan, I can help—"

"No," I interrupt him. Not unless you have a pill to take the pain away.

He sighs, but leaves it. "Ainsley said things didn't go too well in Murdock. I'm sorry that your grandfather is ill."

I nod.

"Where's your backpack and sleeping bag?" he suddenly asks.

"Stolen," I say.

"Dylan, you can't stay out here in this condition," Glen says. "Let me take you to a doctor, or at least to a shelter."

"No." I sway on my feet, and Glen reaches out a hand to steady me.

"Are you taking something?" he asks.

"Painkillers."

Glen grimaces. "From the street? You don't know what you're taking. It could be anything."

But I don't care because *anything* stops the hurting.

Glen switches the briefcase to his other hand. "That boy you're sometimes with. The one who can't keep still . . ."

"Twitch?"

"Yes, that's the one. Do you know his real name?"

I heard it once at Brad's. "It's Aaron, but I don't know his last name. Why?"

Glen looks straight at me. "He took a turn for the worse today."

What's a turn for the worse mean? He's dying? I can't ask.

"The police were around the centre, Ainsley said, wanting to know if anyone knew his name. They want to contact his parents."

I snort at that, and hold my aching sides. "His parents. They won't care. Tell the cops to look at his arms. His step-father used him as an ashtray."

Glen gazes up at the church's spires. "Jesus Christ," he whispers.

It's a prayer, I think.

"I hate this. I hate *this*!" He gestures at me, at the street, the buildings surrounding us. "I had a younger brother who lived on the streets. He had a terrible time in school, and at home he couldn't get along with our parents. They fought all the time. He got into drugs in a big way and landed on the street. I put him into rehab a couple of times, but he OD'd five years ago and died."

"So that's why you do the school thing, donate stuff?" I say. "For forgiveness?"

Glen gives a tight smile. "No," he says. "I don't need to be forgiven. I stopped beating myself up about it last year . . . Sorry." He grimaces. "Bad choice of words. Drugs were his decision, and nothing I could say or do would have stopped him. It took me a long time to realize that it was his choice. But after he died, I did push to get the street school open, and provided supplies and equipment, because I thought maybe I could help some other kid. A kid who was smart and had potential and could make it, given half a chance. A kid like you. I can help you, Dylan. Ainsley, Children's Services, they can all help you if you'll let them, but ultimately, that is your decision. I can't make it for you. You're hurting now, physically and emotionally, but think about what I said."

Help me? Go to school? Shit! He doesn't know what he's talking about. I don't even have a change of underwear. A sliver of soap. I can't start all over again. I'm too fucking tired.

I arrive at the arcade early and wait in the cold. Eventually, the Bandana Kid shows.

"Here you go," he says. He holds out a small plastic bag with four pills.

"How much?"

"Don't worry about it, man," he says.

But I do worry about it. I'll pay for these pills sooner or later. Nothing is for free.

But I need them. "Thanks," I say, and pop one immediately.

"No problem. There's a party tonight. Want to come?"

I don't feel like partying, but he's given me the pills and I haven't paid, so I'm somewhat obligated. Besides, my only other option is returning to the factory.

He takes big strides. I have trouble keeping up with him.

"What's the occasion?" I ask, hoping conversation will slow him down a bit.

He looks at me like I'm nuts. "It's New Year's Eve."

We arrive at an apartment building a few blocks from downtown. Inside, the elevator rises silently, the door slides open, and we go down a hall, footsteps silent on thick carpeting.

"Swanky. Who owns this place?" I ask.

Bandana Kid ignores me.

At the end of the hall, we hear the thump of music. The kid opens a door and a wall of noise greets us. I drift into the apartment in his wake.

It's crowded, hot, and stuffy. Smoke hangs thick and blue in the air and takes on fantastic shapes. I lose the Bandana Kid, but I don't care. The pain has receded, and a platter of crackers and cheese hovers near me. I scoop up a handful and cram them in my mouth. Someone hands me a beer and I drink it in one long gulp, and there's a second one waiting.

"Want to play?" A hand tugs at my pant leg. A red-haired girl smiles up at me. Four people sit with her in a circle, an empty beer bottle in the centre. Before each person is a tiny pile of rainbow-coloured pills.

"It's spin the drug," she says.

I join them.

"Take a turn." She gestures toward the beer bottle.

I spin and it lands on a little pile of yellow tablets. The girl scoops one up. "You have to take it now," she says. "That's the rules." She pops it into my mouth.

The music gets louder, the room gets hotter, and I'm having a great time. No pain, and I discover that I'm a genius when I talk. Everything I say is witty or profound. The red-haired girl hangs on my every word. Einstein would be proud of me.

"I'll be back," I tell her. I wander down a hallway, looking for a washroom.

Raised voices come from behind a door, then a girl crying. Suddenly, it swings open, and Vulture fills the doorway.

"Dylan."

His apartment, his party, his beer, his pills. On some level I knew it, but in my desperation, I buried that reality away.

"Having a good time?"

"Yeah. Great," I tell him.

The door opens wider, and Jenna, tear trails down her cheeks, peers from behind Vulture. "Dylan? What are you doing here?"

"He's joined the party," Vulture says. He wraps an arm around Jenna and pats her ass. "Time to get to work, baby."

"It's so cold out there, Brendan," she complains. "And it's New Year's Eve. Can't I take a break?"

He gives her a small shove out the doorway into the hall.

"New Year's Eve means big bucks, baby. All those guys out there wanting to start the year with a bang." He laughs at his own joke.

Jenna's shoulders slump in defeat. "I just want to talk to Dylan for a minute," she says, with a spark of defiance.

"Sure." He's agreeable. He's got us both where he wants us. He pushes past me and goes down the hall toward the party.

Jenna watches his back disappear, then turns to me. "You don't want to have anything to do with him, Dylan."

Funny, my words, but they're coming out of her mouth.

"What about you?" I ask. "If you know what he's like, why are you still here?"

"I have nowhere else to go."

"Home."

"Home?" Her eyes fill with tears. "Dylan, home is Dad coming into my room at night." She wraps her arms around herself. "He told me he loved me. That's what people who love each other do together. I believed him for a long time. I knew it was wrong, but I believed him. He was my dad."

She tosses her head. "And now I feel real bad because I left, but my sister is still there. I don't know if he'll do the same thing to her."

"Tell someone," I say. "Don't let him get away with it."

"Who'd believe me? A kid. A runaway who's mad at her dad. It's my word against his."

"But you only traded that for this," I say.

"This doesn't hurt as much."

"Hey." Vulture saunters down the hall. "Less talk. More work."

"Bye, Dylan," Jenna says softly.

Chapter 25

The party lasts late into the morning on New Year's Day. Another one starts that evening. Two blessedly painless, stoned days later, I'm still at Vulture's apartment. Finally, people begin to clear out, and by early afternoon there are only two of the Bandana Kids, Jenna, and me left—and a huge mess. My head's a mess, too, fuzzy and throbbing, and my ribs begin to ache.

"Clean this place up," Vulture orders the Bandana Kids. "You." He points at Jenna, who is sprawled on the couch, smoking. "Get some sleep. You look like shit, and you're working tonight. Dylan, come with me."

He leads the way out onto the balcony. Alarm bells ring through the woolly thickness in my head.

"Have a good time?" he asks.

"Yeah. It was okay," I answer carefully.

He lights a cigarette, all the while staring at me.

"About the pills, food, beer," Vulture says. "You can settle up with Lurch. He'll tell you the balance of what you owe me."

He sounds like an accountant.

"If you find yourself short of cash, we have a few odd jobs you could do for us." He takes my chin in his hand and tilts my head first one way, then the other. "You know, you're a good-looking kid, or you would be if you were clean. A bath, some decent clothes, and there'd be people willing to pay top price for you."

Turning tricks. For him.

I yank my head out of his hand, feeling bile rise in my throat.

Vulture leans against the balcony railing, kicks a piece of ice over the edge, and watches it fall. "It's a long way down," he says. "Ground's frozen. A person could get really hurt if he fell." He throws his cigarette over. "We'll set something up. A percentage for you. A larger one for me, of course, as I'll be providing your clothes. Less the money you owe."

"Yeah. Sure, sure," I stammer. Anything to get off the balcony.

"Good. I'm glad we understand each other."

As we go back into the living room, the heat and stink make my head spin. "Help these boys with this." He gestures around the room. "There's a vacuum cleaner in a closet in the back." He grabs a leather coat and heads out the door.

I go down the hall and open a door, thinking it's the closet, but it's a second bedroom, obviously used as storage space. And there is my backpack with my sleeping bag sitting on the floor. I stare at it a moment, then quietly close the bedroom door and go in search of the closet. That life is over. This is my life now.

Dumping the vacuum in the middle of the floor, I crawl behind a couch to find an electrical outlet and come across a little hoard of pills. I pop two, and the rest I squirrel away in my pocket, and suddenly, I'm sick of myself and sick of this room.

I dig my coat out from a pile next to the door. "I'm going out for a bit."

"Hey, Brendan said you were supposed to stay here," says one of the kids.

"He doesn't own me," I say. "Tell him I've changed my mind. I don't want any part of him."

Jenna stabs her cigarette butt into an ashtray, watching me carefully.

"Tell him yourself," the kid says. "You owe him money and he'll get it from you one way or the other. You can run, but he'll find you. Even other cities. He knows people everywhere. Besides, you'll be crawling back looking for more of these." He shakes a little container of pills. "And your girlfriend here won't be able to come through any more. Where do you think she got them in the first place?"

Jenna pushes herself into the couch, avoids looking at me.

"It was Brendan who gave them to her. He knew what he was doing. She knew it, too."

He's lying. I will Jenna to look up at me, let me see in her eyes that he's lying, but she buries her head in her arms.

"You bitch," I say to her.

Her shoulders twitch, but that's the only sign she heard me.

I bend again to the pile of coats and rummage in pockets until I come up with enough change for bus fare.

"You've been had, man," the Bandana Kid shouts as I leave, slamming the door behind me.

Riding the elevator down to the street, I feel numb. How could she do that to me? Out on the street, people's faces float by, indistinct. I need to get some money together, fast. Somehow I find the right bus and stagger up the steps, the pills catching up to me. The driver stares at me, wondering if he should kick me off, but I drop into a seat, and he closes the bus doors. I sit in a stupor, and it is only as we pass Micha and Jordan's school that I move, to pull the cord.

There's a snowman in the yard at the house—Dan's idea, no doubt. I knock the head off it as I pass. This time I don't hesitate but walk straight in.

Cartoon laughter greets me. Micha and Jordan are stretched full length on the floor in front of the television.

"Where is she?" I ask thickly. I won't say Mom.

"Dylan!" Micha runs toward me, but I push him away, too hard, and he falls on his back in the middle of the room. "Sorry. Sorry. They're sore. My . . . my . . ." My tongue feels thick, the words falling from it slurred as I try to explain my hurt ribs.

"Get the hell out of here!" My mother comes into the room.

"I have every right to be here," I shout back.

Jordan turns off the television and huddles with Micha on the floor. It's not often I've seen Jordan scared. He is now.

"You don't belong here any more," my mother yells into the sudden silence.

"You can't just fucking kick me out of your life like that. I'm your son. Look what you've done to me! Look at me!" I scream. "I've got nowhere to sleep, nothing to eat. I got nearly beaten to death . . ."

I turn and I lean my head against the wall, shaking. Why doesn't it matter to anyone that I'm hurt? Why don't I matter?

"What's going on here?"

Dan comes up behind my mother, but he doesn't touch her. He keeps a distance, looking at her, then me. Micha begins to cry noisily and runs to Dan, who puts an arm around him.

"What did I do?" I ask my mother. "What did I do that you hate me for?"

She doesn't answer.

"I said, what is going on?" Dan repeats.

Still she says nothing. The pills, the beer—my stomach churns.

"You're not in any condition to be here," Dan says to me. "You shouldn't be like this in front of the boys."

"I need some money. She owes me that." The sickness comes suddenly. I stagger out the door and heave my guts into the bushes.

They follow me out and Micha wails anew, but now about his broken snowman. Dan pushes the boys back into the house, disappears for a moment, then returns with a box of tissues. I take one and wipe my mouth.

He holds out a ten-dollar bill. "Take this," he says. "Go somewhere and get yourself together. Don't ever come back here drunk or stoned again, because *I* won't let you in. I need some time to talk to Joan and get to the bottom of this. Where can I reach you?"

"Nowhere." I snatch the money from his hand and push past. "Forget it. Tell her I won't be back. Tell Micha . . ." My voice breaks. "Tell him I'm sorry. About his snowman, about—everything."

Chapter 26

In the library's washroom, I sit in a cubicle on the floor, white toilet bowl at eye level. I have no memory of the bus trip downtown, no memory of walking to the library, no memory of coming into this small space and sliding down the wall. There is one thing I remember, though: a phone call. To Glen.

"I need money," I say to him.

"No," he replies quietly.

"I'm in trouble. I owe somebody money. I have to pay it back."

"You owe me money," Glen says.

I'm silent. He's right.

"No one's denying you've been treated badly all around, but now it's time for you to decide what to do for *you*."

"I can't—" I begin.

He interrupts me. "You can. You don't have to do anything big, just take some small steps to make your life better. But only you can make that decision."

"Please, only this one time. I won't ask for money again."

"No."

And he hung up.

Make decisions. You have to have options to make decisions, and I don't have any. I hold his card over the toilet but put it back into my pocket. Climbing to my feet, I push open the stall door and he's there. Einstein.

Perched on the edge of the sink, Einstein peers around the room with a puzzled air. Finally, he focuses on me. "What are you doing to yourself, Dylan?" he asks.

He doesn't say *what*, but *vat*. He runs a hand through unruly hair, making it stand on end. The hair, the baggy-kneed pants, the shapeless jacket and tie, all are askew. He could be one of the library lounge crowd, except for the keen eyes beneath bushy eyebrows.

I shrug.

"Ah. I have a theory about this raising and lowering of shoulders," Einstein begins.

My mouth drops open. "So do I," I say.

"Ah," he says. "You're a man of theories, like myself."

"Except you're a genius and I'm not."

"A genius." Einstein smiles, and creases form around his eyes. "Who's to say what makes a genius? I say I'm a thinker. Always my mind, it goes round and round. Sometimes like a man possessed."

I nod my head sympathetically. "I know what that's like. Your brain all afire."

He crosses his legs, making himself comfortable, settling in for a chat. That makes me uneasy. How long does a hallucination usually stay around?

"So, Dylan, why did you bring me here? How you did it—I'll have to think about later. A most interesting puzzle," he adds. His eyes get a faraway look as he stares at a point above my shoulder.

I clear my throat and he starts.

"I guess you're the result of one of those pills," I say.

"Are you ill? Why are you taking pills?"

"They're painkillers."

"And you are in pain." It's not a question.

I cross to the sink, squirt soap into my hands, and stick them under the faucet. The water turns on.

Einstein jumps off the counter and stares at the stream of water. "How did you do that?" he asks. He bends and examines the tap.

"It's probably got a motion sensor. The toilets flush automatically, too."

Einstein goes into the stall I recently vacated.

"You don't say. Amazing."

"Those usually work with light beams . . ." I stop. What the hell am I doing? I'm explaining technology to a hallucination. "Never mind. Look, Albert. Why don't you just go?" I say.

"You brought me. You have to send me back," Einstein replies reasonably.

"Fine. Go back," I order.

Nothing happens. He's still here. Maybe if I piss him off, he'll leave.

"You know, some of your theories suck," I say.

"What is this word, *suck*?" He puts his hand under the dryer, but it doesn't turn on.

"It means they're bad. Really lousy theories."

Bushy eyebrows rise. "Which ones are you referring to?"

"First, your theory of relativity—"

"Mass and energy are equal, and mass, dimension, and time increase with velocity," Einstein says.

"Yeah, well . . . Want to hear my theory of relativity?"

"Certainly."

"Okay. My theory of relativity is that *relatives* all *suck*." I begin to laugh. "Relativity. Do you get it?" Pain stabs at my ribs as tears run down my cheeks, but I can't stop laughing.

"Relatives as in kinship," Einstein says.

"Yeah, relatives, family, as in my loser father who leaves me before I'm even born, my mother who kicks me out of the house because she wants to pretend she never had me." The laughter turns to sobs that tear from my throat. "And my grandfather who never bothered to look for me."

"$E=mc^2$. Energy equals mass multiplied by the square of the velocity of light. Matter and energy are regarded as equivalents, mutually convertible," Einstein says.

"That guy, Jack, he said Granddad wanted to get custody of me. Why didn't he do it?"

"There is matter, and then there is matter."

"What are you going on about?" I ask impatiently.

"Matter, Dylan. Do you matter, Dylan? To anyone?" He smiles. "My little joke, like yours about relativity."

I can't believe this guy. Why did people think he was a genius? He's a lunatic.

"And you know your other theory, the one you don't actually believe," I go on. "About black holes in space."

"I'm still not convinced they exist," Einstein states.

"Oh, they exist all right. I'm being dragged into one right now. My life is a huge black hole. What is your theory about that?"

A man opens the door, sees me talking, glances around the empty room, and hastily backs out.

"Why are you so wrapped up in theories?" Einstein asks.

That stumps me for a moment. "I guess it's because when I have a theory, it means I have everything figured out. I have everything under control."

He nods. "Yes, it gives the illusion of control, but you can't control everything. No one can.

"I have a theory that I want to share with you," Einstein continues. "A rebuttal, let's say, to your theory of relativity. My theory is that the problem is you."

"What?"

"Perhaps it is you who has a flaw that makes people reject you. Perhaps it is you who *sucks*."

"That's just stupid," I yell. "And what the hell do you know? Your socks don't even match, genius. One is black and one is brown."

"The function of socks is to keep my feet warm. The colour doesn't affect the function," Einstein says.

Footsteps echo in the hall outside the door. The man must have alerted the security guard.

"You can't just say you have a theory that I have a flaw," I tell Einstein. "You have to prove it."

"Very well. Let us look at the evidence. You say you were rejected by your father."

"Hey, I rejected him, so that doesn't count."

"Your mother . . ."

I shrug.

"Your grandfather . . ."

"Jack said he tried to find me. My mother didn't give me his letters. And besides, Grandma had died." Why am I trying to convince him? "Micha and Jordan. My brothers. They like me." My trump card.

"Hmm." Einstein is noncommittal. "Your last visit home wasn't too successful. And Jenna?"

"Well, she's going through her own problems right now," I offer weakly. Jenna did reject me.

"Where did you get such a stupid theory, anyway?" I ask him.

Einstein smiles. "It's yours."

Chapter 27

The door to the washroom opens and the security guard with the caterpillars over his eyes steps in. "You got a problem in here?" he asks.

I whip my head back to Einstein, but he's gone.

"No," I say. "Guess not."

"The library's closing shortly. Time you cleared out," he says, and he escorts me to the door.

I wander the streets, keeping an eye out for Vulture. Eventually, I find myself in a doorway across from the converted church where Brad lives. It's just after midnight, but it's the weekend, and most of the apartments have lights on, including Brad's. Two couples come toward me, and I step out of the doorway to ask for change—there are four of them after all—but I stop myself. I'm finished with theories.

I stare at Brad's apartment window. Twitch said you take a pill and it's easy. I have two pills in my pocket. And Brad has pills. He also has a warm apartment, biscotti, coffee, a tidy bedroom—I shy away from that thought—and hot water. Most important, he has money. I figure if I do it just this once, I can settle my debt with Vulture and be free of him.

I feel a tug on my arm and turn around to see Amber. "I wondered where you got to," she says.

She looks frail tonight, and pathetically young with that bulging belly beneath the too-small coat. She has my toque on her head.

"I've been around," I say.

"You've been at Brendan's."

"Yeah, well, I'm not going back there."

"Fuck, Dylan," she says. "No one's ever broken free of Brendan."

The black hole gets deeper.

"Ainsley is looking for you," Amber continues.

"Why? Does she want to play social worker?"

"Lighten up. Ainsley's okay."

"Yeah. I know."

I glance at the lighted apartment window and she follows my gaze.

"What's up there?" she asks.

"A way to pay off my debt," I reply. I pull her into the shelter of the doorway and wrap my arms around her. "You're cold. You shouldn't be out here. You're going to get sick," I tell her.

"I couldn't face that fucking factory any more," Amber admits. "Especially when you're not there. Or Twitch."

"Have you heard how he is?"

"Ainsley says he's doing better."

"Really? That's great."

She snuggles against me for warmth. It feels absurdly good to have another person that close to me. "Jenna . . ." I begin. I don't know how to go on.

"What about her?" Amber stiffens slightly.

"She screwed me over. When I was in the factory there. Those pills. Brendan gave them to her to give to me, and she knew it."

"Don't be too hard on her," Amber says. "She had no choice. When girls first get out here, they hook up with someone like Brendan. They're so fucking scared and it makes them feel safe. They also think they can walk away from him whenever they want, and then they discover they can't. I know. I've been there. If she tries to leave, he'll beat her up."

"There's got to be an escape."

"Get pregnant like me," Amber says.

"How did Ainsley do it?"

"That woman's got some guts. She fucking clawed her way out. But Jenna, she doesn't have that inside. Brendan will get her into drugs and turning tricks and porno movies. She'll be in so fucking deep, she'll never get out. He takes your self-respect. The life takes your self-respect. And once that's gone, well, you're lost."

Self-respect. I stare up at Brad's window.

"But it's every man for himself out here," Amber says.

"Why did you help me if you believe that?" I ask.

"You? You were so fucking pathetic." She laughs. "I never saw anyone so fucking scared. I couldn't leave you out there looking like that."

"I wasn't that scared," I protest.

"You fucking were."

I look up at Brad's window. It's getting late. If I'm doing anything, it'll have to be soon.

"Does turning tricks get easier over time?" I ask.

"No." She buries her head in the front of my coat. "I try to shut my brain off, you know, pretend it's just a job, but every time I do it, it takes a little more of me. I'm nearly gone, Dylan."

I pull out the ten-dollar bill Dan gave me. "Here. Take this and get a hot dinner."

She doesn't argue, just takes the money. We all need to survive.

"And get something decent to eat. It's better for the baby."

"What are you? The fucking father? I'll see you around." She starts down the street.

"Oh." She turns. "I nearly forgot about Ainsley. Some guy was down at the centre looking for you. His name was Dan. She said if I saw you, to let you know. She said he was your stepfather?"

"My stepfather?"

"That's what she said."

"Okay."

She starts to walk away.

"Thanks—Faith," I call after her.

Stepfather. If he told Ainsley that, then he must know who I am. Who told him? The kids or Mom? I don't know what to think of a stepfather.

A shadow passes by the window of Brad's apartment. What if Brad doesn't want me? I'm flawed. Einstein and his matter? Who do I matter to? Jordan and Micha? Granddad? Did I matter to him? I think I did. But maybe what's important is not that I matter to them, but that they matter to me. And mostly that *I* matter to me.

The lights go off in Brad's apartment and I leave the doorway. As I walk, my brain turns over and over. Finally, I find a pay phone and pull out Glen's card. With shaking fingers,

I insert a coin, dial, and listen to it ring. *It's late, you idiot*, I tell myself. *He's probably asleep.*

"Hello?"

My lips are so frozen they won't work. I panic, because I don't have another quarter if he hangs up.

"Hello?" Glen repeats.

"It's Dylan," I say. "When can I start work?"

Chapter 28

The accepted theory is that once something is sucked into a black hole, it can't escape. I have a theory that something can. Me.

Author's Note

In North America's wealthiest cities, many children go to sleep hungry, live in poverty, or are the victims of family violence and abuse. Many children run away from, or are thrown out of, desperate home situations to live on the streets, where they soon find themselves in dire straits.

Filthy and hungry, they turn to drugs to dull their pain, prostitution and theft to earn money to eat. Pimps and drug dealers take advantage of these vulnerable children. It is a day-to-day struggle to live.

Many of the children are illiterate; as the "regular" school system is unable to deal with them, they drop out. Without education, a fixed address, or clean clothes, they are unemployable. Many of the children have been shunted from foster home to foster home, never fitting in anywhere. Social services, schools, and government agencies fail them. These are difficult children.

There are no pat solutions to the problem of street kids. Various remedies have been tried, from sweeping them under the rug to putting them in group homes, but there are few successes. The most promising solution is to catch the problem before it begins, at the family level, but the agencies who strive to help these children are understaffed and under-funded, and their task overwhelming.

It is important that you, the young adult reading this book today, be aware of that kid on the corner of a city street, the one with an outstretched hand. You will grow up to help run this country and will inherit the problem. We must all work toward a solution.

Acknowledgements

Many thanks to Lynne Missen, children's editor at Harper-Collins Canada, and to my agent, Scott Treimel, for their belief in this book. And a special thank you to my husband, Joe, for sticking with me for thirty years. Happy Anniversary!